Hooch Runners

A Novel

Dianne Zimmermann

Printed in the United States of America.

Cover art by the author.

ISBN 978-1-943650-38-5

Published 2016 by BookCrafters, Parker, Colorado.
BookCraftersColorado@gmail.com

Copies of this book may be ordered from
www.bookcrafters.net
and other online bookstores.

*I dedicate this book to my friends
whose never-ending encouragement
drove me on when the going got tough.*

Acknowledgements

I would like to thank LA Mott
for reading, editing, and offering suggestions
and words of encouragement.

Chapter One

Mary sat on the back porch, in the old creaky rocker, slowly rocking back and forth daydreaming then closing her eyes and dozing off, dreaming of a more exciting life. She had just finished cutting and curling hair for several ladies. She was proud of her work and proud of her beauty parlor and happy that she stood up to her husband Beau and insisted that he allow her to turn the large front bedroom they never used into a beauty parlor. He had resisted at first until she convinced him that it would bring in extra money. Mary had a secret motive of course and that was not only to contribute to the household expenses. She also saved money in an envelope hidden way in the back of her dresser drawer for herself. Having her own money made her feel strong. She was happy that she had accepted the invitation from her hairdresser, Judy, to train her and sell her equipment to her, because she and her husband were going to pack up and sell their house and move to Indiana to Judy's family farm. In six months Mary was trained and took over Judy's clientele. Mary enjoyed being a beauty operator it gave her a sense of accomplishment and independence.

After working all day, it was nice to sit on the back porch, relax, take a nap, and then tend to her mending. She tried to concentrate on her stitching, but as she looked around, she was bothered by the fact that the porch needed painting. Most of the paint had peeled off the floor, the posts, and the ceiling. She was going to have to go to the hardware store and buy paint and paint the porch herself. She already knew Beau would never get around to it. She cut the grass; she had already given up on trying to get Beau to do that. She had to admit that she paid more attention to details and was more particular than he. She wished Beau had an interest in things around the house, but he didn't. He said he had no time to do chores and fix things. But Mary knew his main interest was his hunting cabin in the woods up in the bluffs. He called the cabin his escape place. Mary told Beau that she felt as if she needed an escape place herself and waited for Beau to invite her to ride along up to the cabin but, Beau told her that women were not allowed in the cabin; only he and his brother were permitted access, he proudly boosted. Beau had made that point very clear on more than one occasion, when she wanted to tag along. The answer was always a plain and simple, no and her feelings would get hurt. Mary knew Beau and his brother, Jess, were cooking hooch up there on that mountaintop and guessed they didn't want her to get in the way.

As she sat and looked at the faded paint, Mary felt a bit like faded paint herself. She felt old and eternally stuck in her situation. The future was so predictably bleat, she felt at times. She pushed herself to ignore her feelings and continue to carefully stitch the tear in her Sunday dress. She was particular and gingerly pulled each stitch carefully through the material, in order to do a neat and tidy job. As she worked, she thought about her life so far living in Marysville.

She had been happy enough when they first got married, she guessed; as happy as can be expected living in a small country town that felt as if it stood still in time. Nothing ever changed there in Marysville, each day was the same old pace, and she felt as if something was missing. Mary had always dreamed of living a more adventurous life in a growing bustling community, where there were more stores, restaurants and theatres and things to do. She felt a little sad as she sat alone rocking, head lowered, straining her eyes to see each tiny stitch, in the shadows of late afternoon, as she concentrated on mending her dress. She had torn her dress last Sunday in church, when she caught it on a nail that was sticking out on the side of the pew. She made a mental note to stick a hammer in her pocketbook and take it along to Sunday's service, so she could hammer that nail back down. She didn't understand why the men folk of the congregation could not fix things like protruding nails. But, they were men after all, and men needed to be asked, and then the men folk would get around to it whenever it suited them; that is, unless they forgot first and Beau always forgot, but he never forgot to do things for Jess.

Mary was jealous and felt that Beau's brother, Jess, always came first, and she last. She was angry, because it seemed that men could do whatever they wanted to do, they could be adventurous and take chances. Women on the other hand were expected to be docile, pretty and polite and behave in certain ways; there were limits to their expectations and professions, each expecting to be stay-at-home wives and mothers. Mary dreamed of adventures.

Beau and his brother, Jess did what they wanted to do, and that was distill hooch. Beau and his brother, Jess, smelled of booze all the time. The only thing that Mary could figure was that the sheriff was letting them get away with it. You would think that the sheriff would wonder where they got their booze. But the sheriff only had one deputy and talk was that they could not keep up with all the hidden breweries and distilleries popping up all over the countryside. Speakeasies and back alley gin joints, or so Mary had heard the ladies in her beauty parlor say were all the rage now. They wanted their hair done in the latest bobs, with big curls coming out onto their cheeks and down on their foreheads. She envied those partying folks she and Beau never partied.

Beau was conservative and a lot like Mary's daddy, and probably why she fell in love and married him, she guessed. That and the fact that he would not take no for an answer and asked her to marry him over and over again, until she said yes. He said that he was madly in love with her ever since they were kids and walked to school together. Beau was a clever fellow and after school, when he walked her home and they got to her house, he would strike up small talk with her folks. He hung around chitchatting until supper was put on the table and Mary's folks invited him to stay.

Mary was deep in thought as she stitched her dress, she was happy that her dress could be mended and made presentable. She was all but finished mending now. If only her life, she thought, could be mended that easily. Her gloomy thoughts continued on as she sat on the porch putting off going inside to start fixing supper, she knew Beau would be home soon and hungry, but she just couldn't muster up the energy to get up and get things started. They would have the left over stew from last nights' supper she figured. She usually spooned out small portions with lots of bread, to make it last and to stretch the few dollars they had.

They had to watch each nickel and dime they spent. Beau promised to bring home money, as soon as he and his brother, Jess, made this week's hooch run. He told her that he had a lot of money owed him, and he planned on collecting it on this run. The plan was for Beau and Jess to break even on the cost of building another distillery next to the one they already had in the hidden cellar of the cabin. Right before he died, Beau's dad dug a dandy secret cellar in the cabin he had built several years prior. The cellar had thick concrete walls and a hidden opening in the main floor of the cabin and another hidden opening on outside of the cabin; which was hidden under the low branches of a cluster of pines trees. The lid to the cellar was concealed by fallen pine needles. It was the perfect setup.

"Mary, where are you?" Beau hollered from the front of the house. He wanted to eat supper before he and Jess headed up North to deliver a truckload of hooch filled jugs.

"I'm on the back porch," Mary yelled back. She could hear her husband holler for her. She thought by now he should had learned to always go look for her because she wasn't going to stop what she was doing to jump up and run to him to find out what he wanted. He always yelled! She could never understand why he just did not walk around to the back and look for her, instead of all that yelling. Right after they got married when he yelled like that, she would jump up to go find him and see what he wanted, but no more. He could just come find her. They had been married for three years and as many miscarriages, and she was just getting tired and crabby and she knew it. So, she fought the urge and made up her mind that she was not getting up besides: she only had three or four more stitches to do to finish mending her good dress and she did not want to break her stitching stride. Anyway, that was her excuse today. Her mending was a work of art of perfection, just like her hair styling and could not be interrupted.

"Oh there you are," smiled Beau, as he rounded the corner to the back of the house. He was happy and in a good mood because he was getting ready to make a hooch delivery with his brother, Jess. Mary was not at all crazy about Jess but she knew that she had to tolerate him for Beau's sake. Jess was an angry man and took his anger out on everyone around him especially his wife, Joan. He liked to smack her around in public; it made him feel like a man. It made her feel ashamed and embarrassed like a whipped dog. Mary only wondered what he might have done to her in the privacy of their home and wondered if Joan was telling her everything. Joan would wait until there were no customers in Mary's beauty parlor then come in crying. Jess did not know it yet, but Joan wasn't only sad, she was getting angry, and swore to Mary that she would get him back on day. Joan told Mary that Jess just threw one to many punches to suit her. Jess was a big brute and didn't only push Joan around; he liked to pick fights with the townspeople and most learned to steer clear of him. Joan had her complaints about Jess, and Mary had her complaints about Beau so together they would sit in Mary's beauty parlor and cry and console each other. Mary thought Beau was in awe of his older brother, Jess, just as Jess had been in awe of his dad. She felt that both Jess and their dad were bad influences for Beau.

Beau's dad had begun building a distillery on rumors about prohibition becoming law, long before it became law. He got as far as getting the cabin and cellar build then ran out of money, and that was why he had to rob the bank. Beau and Jess's father and mother were bank robbers and died in a shootout with county sheriffs.

Beau took it better than his older brother. Jess missed his folks terribly and in his sorrow drank a lot and was drunk all the time. He drank up most of the booze that they distilled. Of course Jess's excuse was that he had to sample the booze to make sure it was fit to sell. He said it had to be exceptional, otherwise their lives would be in danger from angry disappointed customers. Beau drank his share, too. They were happily in the hooch distilling business and having more fun than two hogs swaddling in a mud puddle.

Beau and Jess were as sober as sober could possibly be for them, after sampling their product as they loaded up the truck with gallon jugs. They had to make sure the jugs were hidden and packed well between straw bales. They did not want any jugs to break and waste their precious booze. And they didn't want booze dripping out of the truck bed and smelling up the countryside as the sheriff patrol cars passed them and there were more and more of them on the roadways since Prohibition became law. Jess and Beau weren't the only distillers in the county and the hooch competition was becoming stiff. The major roadways had lots of traffic, so Jess and Beau switched to taking the back roads between towns to get to their customers in order to avoid the competition and the law and sometimes get away from drunken angry customers.

"We're getting ready to head out now, Mary," smiled Beau showing the space where his front tooth once was. A dissatisfied buyer who thought he was over charged knocked it out. As the buyer argued with Jess and Beau his pal grabbed the jugs and refused to pay. Jess took the first swing then ducked as the angry customer swung an axe handle and narrowly missed Jess's face and struck Beau right in the mouth. His front tooth broke off and cut his lip leaving an ugly scar behind. A reminder to duck, Jess warned, then laughed every time he looked at Beau's crooked smile. Beau was self-conscious and either did not smile or covered his mouth with his hand when he did.

"We got the back of the truck all loaded up and we're ready to hit the road," announced Beau.

"Better watch out for Sheriff Cooper, he has been out looking for hooch runners today, is the talk around town," warned Mary handing Beau a bag of sandwiches while walking him to the door. Mary looked up and down the street to make sure the sheriff was nowhere in sight.

Mary and Beau lived in the middle of town in his folk's old house. After Beau's folks died they moved out of the apartment and into their house. Beau worked during the week at the gas station pumping gas and working on cars and spent the weekends at the cabin distilling hooch with Jess.

Beau and Jess's folks were shot dead as they ran from the law, Sheriff Cooper told Beau and Jess that sheriffs only planned to question them and that their pappy panicked and started shooting first. But, Beau and Jess were not buying any of it, they thought the sheriff was trigger-happy and had it in for their pappy, none of which, they could prove, of course. The boys could not figure out why their folks did not hide in the mountain cabin. It would have been the perfect hiding place because, no one knew about it. They thought maybe their pappy was protecting the cabin and keeping it a safe hiding place for them. Their pappy had built the log cabin years back, from trees cut down to make the clearing for it. The cabin was nestled high up the wooded mountainside, high near the top, hidden by tall pine trees. The only way to get to the cabin was to turn off the county road, drive a short distance on a grassy field road that looked like it ended by a wooded area and creek. It appeared that the field road was just used for get farm machinery to the back area of the field. But the secret was to drive through the rocky creek at an angle to the other side toward a hidden twisting road that led up through the woods, to the cabin. You had to know that it was there; otherwise you would not see it.

Jess and Beau were angry because the sheriff had accused their pappy of robbing the bank in the next county. The brothers told the sheriff that they were mad because their pappy and mama were dead now, killed needlessly, they had to be innocent because no money was found. Beau and Jess knew better, their pappy was smart; he had already given the stolen bank money to Beau to hide in the hidden distillery cellar in the mountain cabin. Beau and Jess clung to their claim that the sheriff had it in for their dad because their dad had a bad temper, picked fights and cheated in card games. Jess swore the sheriff just wanted to get his mean spirited pappy out of the way.

Beau and Mary lived in an apartment above the old saloon at the time of the shooting and heard the shots. They ran down the street in the direction of Beau's folks' house and found both of them dead. The sheriff told the boys that their pappy shot first and they fired back, and their mama got in the way of the shooting. The sons thought it was nothing more than a cold-blooded double murder committed by the sheriff and his deputies, and because they were the law, they got away with it. Joan, Jess's wife, did not know what to think, she wasn't use to having a thought of her own, because Jess wouldn't allow it. Joan had come to settle into her depession. She had no friends to confide in except for Mary, the only friend Jess allowed her to have.

Mary was sympathetic toward Joan because she was in the same situation but in a lesser degree. Beau had not become abusive toward Mary but she was leery and afraid that if something went very wrong it could set him off and he would become just like Jess. She was afraid that Beau had his dad's temper too, but could control it better. Mary did not know what to think of the whole affair of Jess and Beau's parents' death. She had no opinion of their guilt or lack of guilt. She had grown numb and wished she could move to Floraville.

Mary had no family except for her sister, Ruth, who lived in Floraville, about fifteen miles away in the next county. Mary and her sister Ruth kept in touch by mail. Mary looked forward to her sister's letters, and would get them out of the mailbox before Beau got home. Beau never wanted to visit Ruth so she kept news from Ruth to herself. Beau's excuse for not wanting to visit Ruth was that he was a homebody, so he said. To Mary's disgust, he was no homebody when it came to running hooch. Mary complained to Joan about Beau's stubbornness and Joan complained to Mary about Jess's temper and his threats to beat her.

After a while Jess's threats turned into shoves, then punches to the stomach where bruising was not visible. Mary told her each time she came into the beauty parlor that she should get the hell away from him.

"I just have a bad feeling about Jess," warned Mary. Her intuition told her that she should warn Joan that Jess's temper was only going to get worse if she just kept sitting back and taking it.

"I know, but what can I do? I have no money and no place to go. And nowhere to get any help. I only make a little bit of money working at the dry goods store," cried Joan.

"Well, just keep putting money back for yourself and keep it in a safe place. You can always drive over to my sister's place in Floraville and stay there. Just drive north on Route Thirteen, you'll get there eventually. Just stay on thirteen till you get there." Mary repeated in an attempt to etch the directions into Joan's troubled mind.

"How? I have no way to get there. The damn car is broke down and Jess won't fix it. He uses the truck all the time. He says he doesn't need the car," complained Joan, "I thought about buying a car and keeping it a secret, but that will never work, since I don't have enough money to buy a car. And besides, everyone in town knows Jess, and they would say something to him."

Mary gave Joan her sister's address in Floraville and information about the bus schedule, just in case she would need to get away in a hurry one day.

"Memorize the address and keep a bag packed and be ready to go," she told her then went on to tell Joan about problems of her own.

"Sheriff Cooper sticks his nose in here all the time," Mary said in a tone that reflected her annoyance.

"He comes in here all the time to check on me, so he says." Mary said, "I wish he wouldn't come in here all the time with his flirty ways."

"Well, what do you do when he comes in?" asked Joan getting comfortable in Mary's styling chair. She always looked forward to going to the beauty parlor. It was her one special treat that always brightened her spirits.

"I am about as friendly, as I can bring myself to be," sighed Mary. "He makes me feel uncomfortable, so I just go with it and try to get him out of here as soon as I can, "Mary explained while looking at Joan's reflection in the mirror as she looked up from trimming Joan's neckline. She held her comb and scissors proudly. She was talented at styling hair, and it gave her great satisfaction to be so creative. Ladies would see her work and want her to style their hair too. Her customers were walking advertisements for her.

"Oh, I'm going to love my new bob," smiled Joan.

"It's the latest fashion craze," smiled Mary "I saw it in the *Ladies Home Journal*."

After she finished cutting Joan's hair, Mary went on and finger-waved her new hairdo. Joan was happy with her new bob. It was all the rage, just as was dancing the jive and Muddy Waters jazz. The sisters-in-law enjoyed their times together catching up on what their husbands were up to, and the latest gossip of Marysville. But, they wanted to have fun too, and wished that they had a speakeasy where they could get all dressed up and dance and have fun, even if their stick-in-the-mud husbands did not want to, they'd go.

Chapter Two

Marysville was a small town of about nine hundred people and located in southern Illinois. It was nearly one hundred miles to Springfield. Mary knew that the Beau and Jess would be gone for several days because they made delivery stops all along the way to just south of Springfield. People in that area liked Beau and Jess's hooch and word traveled fast for good booze during prohibition years. The Feds and police in the larger municipalities had more manpower, so Beau and Jess stayed away and only had hooch customers south of Springfield.

Mary didn't mind being home alone while Beau was gone. She had beauty parlor customers to keep her busy and made sure she filled up her appointment book to keep busy so she could make and save a lot of money. She wanted a monetary safety net in case Beau never came back from one of those dangerous road trips, and she could go live with her sister Ruth in Floraville.

What Beau did was dangerous and against the law and it was her job, so he instructed, to keep what he did secret. She hated lying, watching and weighting every word she spoke to cover for Beau each time he went on the road to make deliveries. Each time Beau left, she wondered if it would be his last time — maybe a hotheaded customer, the law, or his crazy brother's temper might get him killed. Mary had to prepare herself for Beau's death because she felt his death was inevitable, her intuition had warned her. She felt terrible for thinking that, and never told anyone, not Joan, not even her sister, Ruth, in one of her weekly letters, because she thought it sounded like wishful thinking. She worried about being married to Beau. She worried if he could become angry and mean like his brother Jess had become. She knew that she should leave Beau and maybe one day she would; after all, she had her own way of making money and knew that she could support herself if she had to. She always put money aside just like she told Joan to do, because you just never know what might happen.

***

On January 16, 1920, Prohibition came into effect after the propelled efforts by the anti-alcohol league. Across the United States all saloons, breweries and distilleries were locked and boarded up. By 1922 illegal hooch was in full swing being sold all over the countryside. People wanted their alcoholic beverages. Beau and Jess

Jones were young entrepreneurs and wanted in on the action. Their pappy, Hank Jones had distilled booze and his legacy lived on through his sons, they were proud to carry it on. They knew their pappy's distillery formulas, and were ready to cash in on the action. Word got around quick in those days and their pappy's reputation preceded their potential for success. The boys were doing what they loved to do. They distilled and delivered the hooch themselves and made regular runs every week or two.

Tonight was no different and their truck was loaded and ready to go. A neighboring distillery was discovered by the law and blown up in the process of an arrest. That distillery was out of business and so their production was up to meet the demands. Most people thought the Prohibition Law was stupid and had no intention of obeying it.

***

The old Model T truck toddled along the bumpy roadway. Beau had trouble keeping the load on the road when the truck got to swinging back and forth.

"Slow down man!" Beau demanded while was hanging on for dear life.

"I'm doing the best I can," hollered Jess, griping the steering wheel with all his might. When the front wheels hit a big hole in the rutted road, the steering wheel just about jerked right out of his hands. Jess slowed down the old truck, Jess wasn't sure of its age — it's hard to tell when you steal them and all Model T's looked pretty much alike.

"Got to be careful around here. Over yonder behind those trees, is where the sheriff sat last time, remember," warned Beau, "so slow down." Jess didn't slow down but he turned off the main highway and got onto a narrow county road so he would look like a local farmer and not someone just speeding through the area, like he was doing. The back road took them out of their way, but they both thought it was less conspicuous.

Finally, they came to the first customer stop. Bud and his boys were sitting on the front porch smoking pipe tobacco and drinking what little whiskey they had left from Jess and Beau's last hooch run.

"Hello boys," Jess yelled out the window as they pulled up in the yard and the guys yelled back and walked towards the truck.

"I got two jugs for you Bud, hope that will do," said Beau.

"How much?" Bud grunted through yellow teeth. He spit and added, "Here's two empties for you boys."

"You know how much," Beau responded in a stern voice, and was happy to see that Bud had money and was willing to pay. Jess took the two empties from Bud. He got two jugs and handed them to Bud and then got into cab and they headed down the road again. It was best to keep moving, before Bud got any wild ideas about was something to watch out for, it was the customers who could be ornery and not want to pay.

***

The next few stops were without any troubles or complaints from customers. They were getting close to the end of the day and beginning to breathe a slight sigh of relief, but they breathed too soon. Trouble was approaching.

Beau was driving as they came upon a sheriff's car parked in the tall brush along the side of the road. They drove slowly and weren't doing anything wrong. They got almost a half mile away before the sheriff's car pulled out and followed them. He speeded up until he got closer, and then the siren came on.

"Ah hell," Beau turned around and saw the car fast approaching. He did not notice Jess reach for the rifle that was propped between the passenger seat and the door. The sheriff's car was gaining on them. Beau was going as fast as he could, holding tight to the jerking steering wheel, as well as trying to hold his foot steady on the gas pedal as they bounced down the road in the rickety truck. As they approached a bridge that crossed a big river, Beau heard a loud bang. He thought the truck backfired, but then he saw the sheriff's car suddenly swerve. In a billowing cloud of dust the sheriff's car veered off the road, down the embankment and bounced and tumbled down into the river. Beau slowed to a stop just as the sheriff's car hit the water. The river was high and swift and the sheriff's car twisted and jerked against fallen tree limbs and over big rocks then sank in a matter of minutes. They assumed the sheriff perished with the patrol car.

"Oh, he's gone," shouted Jess with confidence, and then laughed an evil laugh that Beau had never heard before, and it frightened him to hear it. *Who was this man sitting next to him*, he thought. Beau was worried that Jess's drinking had turned him into a mean and bitter man.

"Wow, what happened?" asked Beau. "Did a wheel come off?" But as soon as he said it, he saw Jess with rifle in hand sticking his head back into the truck cab. A faint cloud of smoke and the smell of gunpowder filled the cab and Beau realized that Jess had shot at the sheriff's car.

"Oh man," yelled Beau over the noise of the engine, "what the hell you go and do that for?"

"Hey, he's gone," yelled Jess as he grinned and took a swig of hooch from a jug he kept close by. "Well, we don't have to worry about him anymore," Jess mumbled angrily as he wiped his dripping chin with his dirty shirtsleeve. He had no idea he could possibly hit anyone trying to aim a rifle while riding in the bumpy truck; it had to be a freak accident. Maybe a wheel did come loose on the sheriff's car. Either way, they were almost finished with their route for the day and they were glad.

They drove a few more miles, found what looked like a nice secluded spot in the woods and parked behind some trees and slept for a spell. The next day their deliveries were uneventful, except for one guy who did not want to pay the amount they asked. But in the end, he saw things Jess's way, when Jess pointed his gun in his face. They got the heck out of that farm, making sure they weren't being followed. That night they again pulled over, hid the truck and turned off the lights. They slept on the straw in the bed of the truck.

That was how they did their deliveries. When they got too tired to drive, they parked the truck in the woods and slept, or when they were lucky enough to be invited by friendly folks, stayed at customer's farm. Some would let them sleep in their barns. Some of their customers even fed them supper. Whatever their sleeping arrangements were, Jess kept the rifle handy and slept with one eye open, or they took turns keeping guard. One thing for sure, selling hooch was adventurous and never dull, and they were always glad to get back to their own homes.

Chapter Three

Mary kept busy in the beauty parlor while Beau was away on the road or at his cabin. She cut hair and styled the latest finger wave styles with little curls combed forward onto cheeks, and down on foreheads. It was mid-afternoon on the fifth day Beau had been gone, that Sheriff Cooper stopped by the beauty parlor. He saw through the window that she was alone.

"Hello, Mary, say I wonder if you can tell me where Beau is?" The thin tall sheriff said as he stood in the doorway holding the door open. He looked smart in his tan sheriff's uniform. He stood there staring at her, looking her up and down, which gave her a creepy feeling. She wished there was at least one customer in the beauty parlor with her. His uniform hat was pulled down near his eyebrows. The name Cooper was stitched on his shirt pocket.

"Well, I'm not sure where Beau is," answered Mary, smiling a slight smile, while folding a damp towel over the rod near her styling station before turning to give the sheriff her full attention. "I believe he said something about helping his brother," Mary offered and hoped that it sounded convincing enough. She got tired of covering for Beau and Jess. She got tired of lying and trying to remember the stories she had already told the sheriff in his prior visits. She wasn't a storyteller and it got harder and harder not to get the stories all messed up. She hoped her distress did not show through her forced smile as the sheriff looked at her inquisitively before he went on:

"Well, I stopped at the gas station and the new guy there didn't know where he was, so I wondered if you did." He smiled and tipped his hat as he turned to leave. Mary had met eyes with this sheriff before at the lunch diner across the street. He smiled and flirted with her then, and Mary believed that he was trying to flirt with her now. She wasn't real happy about that, but she did not want him to press harder as to the whereabouts of Beau. She thought it was better to play along a little bit with the sheriff, so she smiled back and acted as if she was flattered. She thought that it was the least she could do and it was harmless; she was just being friendly. Besides, her intuition told her that she just might need his help one day, so be friendly.

"Well, I just wondered where he was, hadn't seen him around in a while," Cooper said.

It was plain to see that Sheriff Cooper was more interested in getting to know her better, rather than wonder about where her husband was and what he was up to. *Who knows*, Mary thought, *he probably flirted with all the ladies when their husbands weren't around.*

"Well Mary, I'll be on my way now. I see my deputy just pulled up, must be something going on. Have a nice day," he smiled, tipped the brim of his hat, then turned and walked out the door leaving Mary to wonder just where Beau and Jess were.

It was about an hour later when Mary was busy cutting a lady's hair that Beau stuck his head in the beauty parlor door. He was embarrassed standing there all dirty and stinky so he briefly nodded hello to Mary and the lady, then left to walk around the house and go in the back door to get himself cleaned up.

Mary was glad to see Beau back home safe; but she had to admit that she was a little afraid of him and treaded lightly around him, as to not cross him. She wasn't sure why she was a little afraid of Beau. She figured that fear was contagious and guessed that Joan put those fearful thoughts into her head, because Joan was afraid of Jess. Just how much Beau was like his older brother, she wasn't sure. She wondered when Beau was going to get as mean with her as Jess was to Joan. She thought it was just a matter of time, because tempers ran wild in his family.

Beau's dad was always picking fights, especially after no one was allowed to drink anymore and he was mad about it. The saloons closed up or turned into restaurants or churches; there was no telling how long prohibition would last—maybe forever. But people were attracted to things they liked and even more to things they could no longer get easily, so the hooch popularity was growing.

Later at supper, Mary asked Beau how things went on his delivery route. He merely stated nothing much happened and they got all the hooch delivered to their customers. She was trying hard to engage Beau in conversation, but he was not responding. When Mary asked about Jess, Beau said , Jess had gone on to his house. When Mary thought of Jess, she just wished Jess would treat his wife better. She felt bad for her but listened to Joan and her woes about her abusive husband every time she saw her.

Mary was clueless as far as Jess was concerned. She had no idea Jess still had feelings for her when he married Joan, out of spite, after Mary married his younger brother, Beau. He asked Mary to marry him when they were teenage kids, way before Beau started walking her home from school. She made light of Jess's flirting because she was a little afraid of him. There was just something about him, which made her feel uncomfortable, even back then. Her intuition had warned her something was not right about Jess, there was a hidden evil about him that could erupt at any time.

When Beau started hanging around, she liked him much better than Jess. Beau wasn't at all like Jess, and he and Mary just hit it off right away. Beau was crazy about Mary, and would not take no for an answer when he asked her out, and she liked him too. The third time he asked Mary out, she no longer worried about Jess's feelings and went with Beau. Jess was mad and a sore loser. He did not like to lose to his younger brother, and Jess was revengeful.

Chapter Four

Jess and Joan lived down the street from Beau and Mary, their home was not a happy home, and there were heated arguments. Jess was tired and angry when he got home from the booze delivery, and this time it seemed that he was more short-tempered than usual. Jess had demanded dinner immediately and slammed his fist on the kitchen table. Joan jumped with fright.

"I didn't know when you were going to get home," she said in her defense, taking a step back away from him. As soon as she said it, she knew she shouldn't have. In his mind she was talking back to him. Joan was afraid and did not like the wild angry look in his eyes. His look was evil, much more evil than she had ever seen it. He was drunk. Just as always, he was drunk, but this evening he seemed even more sinister.

She hurried and fried up some ham and potatoes and cooked some green beans for him. She was afraid and avoided him while she cooked and he drank. She quickly set the table and had dinner ready within minutes. He ate like a wild man, stuffing forks full of food in his mouth and chewing noisily. When he was finished, he staggered to the bedroom to sleep. When Joan went to bed a few minutes later, she stayed very quiet and laid on the edge of the bed as far away from him as she could. She had not bothered to undress, for fear she would make noise undressing and wake him up. She just lay there not moving. She felt like running away, but stayed there in her own dark prison, crying while she listened to him snore.

Something woke Jess up in the middle of the night. He was still drunk, and yelled at Joan and accused her of making noise. He rose up and turned to take a swing at her. She jumped up and ran through the kitchen to the back door nearly tripping over a kitchen chair he pushed in her way. He narrowly missed tripping her.

"You bitch!" he hollered and lunged at her. He grabbed her by the waist and spun her around. He pushed her against the kitchen cabinets so hard she knocked her head on the cupboards and she nearly blacked out. In one swift motion he wrapped both his hands around her neck and squeezed shaking her head back and forth. She couldn't breathe and tried to ply his hands loose, but couldn't even get a grip.

Her eyes grew big with fright, loss of breath and disbelief. *What was he doing?* She tried to talk, but couldn't make a sound. Her throat hurt. She tried again to pry his hands apart and away from her neck, but it was no use. With one hand he squeezed her throat, and with the other hand reached behind her and picked up the heavy iron skillet. He managed to raise it up over his head and come down with it. She jerked her head to the side and the skillet almost missed her but nipped the side of her head knocking her unconscious. She slowly slumped down against the cabinets onto the floor. She was bleeding and blood ran from the top of her head, over her face and dripped down onto her light colored cotton dress.

He was certain she was dead, and in his rage of anger, he was glad she was dead. He looked at her slumped there on the floor and for a moment felt nothing. He only thought about the mess he had to clean up and what he was going to have to do with the body. Jess's hand shook as he wiped the blood off the floor and the skillet with the hem of her dress that fanned out around her. He placed the skillet back on the counter top. He was shaking a bit as he rose up to a standing position and began to pace back and forth in the kitchen.

What the hell was he going to do with her? He thought, for a minute. *She was dead.* An idea came to him then, he would go fishing. Yeah, he would go fishing, like he always does. He ran out to his truck and pulled out the big canvas sheet he kept there. He brought it into the kitchen and laid it out next to her, then dragged her body on to it and rolled the canvas up, around her body. When he had her tied in a nice neat bundle, he lifted her up, threw her over his shoulder and carried her outside, and put her in the back of his truck. He made sure he had his fishing gear and drove down to the river. It was near dawn, the time he usually went fishing, the time when the fish were hungry and biting the best. This was good he thought, I'm just doing what I always do, going fishing at dawn. The river was about a mile from the house so it only took him a few minutes to get there, he drove past his usual fishing spot to a more secluded area of the riverbank.

He got out of the truck, looked around and then removed the canvas wrapped body from the truck bed. He laid it on the ground and unwrapped the canvas around her. Looking at her face, quiet and still now, he felt nothing. He merely went about dragging a fallen tree limb over and wrapped fishing line around it and her body. When he thought it was secure enough, he pushed, shoved and rolled it down the embankment into the river.

He was not surprised that he felt no remorse. In fact, killing her was easy. Just as shooting at the sheriff had been easy, and watching his car go down the embankment into the river was easy. Getting rid of Joan was so easy that Jess smiled as he watched her body bob and twist in the swift current of the muddy river. He could see she was beginning to sink as her body rounded the bend out of sight. The water, fish and animals would take care of her remains. But, if someone did find her body, it would look like she had been walking along the path near the river, slipped and fell in, and got tangled up in fishing line and drowned. He stood there for a few seconds after she was gone, out of his life, finally. She did nothing but piss him off anyway.

He laughed out loud, an evil laugh, as he walked back to the truck and got his fishing pole baited then stood on the bank and fished. He smiled and drank hooch out of a jug. He fished until it was time to go to work at the feed store.

In 1922 the laws in favor of women were few. Most women did not drive, few voted although the law was recently passed in 1920 with Constitutional Amendment Twenty allowing women to vote. If a woman did vote she was expected to follow her husband's political advice, because men were more keen on political issues and so convinced their wives that they knew better about such matters. A woman was under a man's thumb, and if he decided to treat her badly, then so be it. The rule of thumb was an understanding: the rod he struck her with be only as round as his thumb, no bigger. Women had their place and were considered second place citizens and fully expected to obey their husbands till death do they part, one way or another, sometimes with a little help from their husbands.

Chapter Five

Mary was busy in her beauty parlor. She looked at her appointment book and saw that Joan was due to come in for a haircut and style in a few minutes. Mary usually set more time aside and spread out appointments when Joan was coming in, so that they would have time to talk about their husbands. The time passed by as Mary straightened up, and washed up combs and brushes. Still, Joan did not show up. She figured that Joan was just running late, maybe she was with a customer at the dry goods store and couldn't leave just yet. There were enough things for Mary to do while she waited. She swept the floor, gathered towels to be washed all the while she wondered what could be holding up Joan. Her intuition told her something was very wrong. She had a few minutes before her next customer was due to arrive, so she hurried and walked to the dry good store to try to find out if Joan came into work that morning.

"Hi Mary, haven't seen you for a while, what brings you in today?" asked Marge, the store owner. "Is there anything I can help you with?" Marge asked as she looked up from her paperwork.

"Just looking around," answered Mary, "I had a few minutes between customers and thought I would come and see if you got in anything new."

"No, everything on display is pretty much the same as last week when you were in the store," answered Marge with a concerned tone. "I have some boxes in the back that need to be opened. They are filled with some lovely dresses, and patterns, bolts of fabrics, and sewing notions. I haven't gotten around to opening the boxes and emptying them yet. You know end of month's bills must be paid first of all," Marge said and sounded aggravated. "And Joan did not show up this morning. I sure could have used her help today." Marge complained as she pushed her glasses up on her nose, and then looked down again at her bookkeeping.

Hearing what Marge said about Joan, Mary knew her face went white. She kept her head down and pretended to look around at some folded sweaters on the table. That was it. Marge said Joan never showed up for work. Guess Marge never thought about Joan and Mary being sisters-in-law and asking Mary if she had seen Joan. Mary didn't say anything and thought it better left alone. Besides the opportunity had passed, as Marge went right back to adding up her bills and scratching figures down in her ledger. Mary thought about interrupting her, but then a woman entered the store and asked Marge questions about some thread and material. Mary just gave up and decided to leave. She slipped out the door and quickly walked back to her beauty parlor just as her next hair appointment was coming up the sidewalk from the other direction. The mystery of Joan's whereabouts was moved to the back of her mind, as Mary got busy.

Several days passed by without an appearance by Joan. Mary was afraid for Joan, but did not know what to do. No one mentioned a thing, and Mary was afraid to ask for fear Jess would come after her if he found out she was snooping round in their business. None of her customers who might have known Joan said anything. Beau never said if Jess had mentioned anything about Joan's whereabouts. Of course, Beau worked at the garage during the day and Jess worked at the feed store, and on weekends, they both went up to the cabin to distill hooch. Nothing was mentioned about Joan, and Mary was afraid to ask. In her gut, her intuition, told her that something very wrong had happened to Joan. Finally after a week had passed, Mary walked over to the dry goods store. Again, Joan was not working in the store. Mary noticed that there were new items on the racks and new material bolts she had not seen the week before. She was curious and looked at them closer.

"Oh, I see some new things," said Mary casually, while she looked around the store. Marge was busy with a couple of customers who were deciding on material and dress patterns. Marge didn't even hear her comment. Mary looked around a bit more and then left to go back to her beauty parlor. Her heart was racing. She should go to Jess and Joan's house, but she was afraid to go there—afraid of what she might find and frankly she was afraid of Jess. It was just odd that she never heard anything about Joan. But, maybe she was the only one concerned,

Mary returned her beauty parlor just as Sheriff Cooper walked by, and tipped the brim of his service hat in greeting. "Good afternoon ma'am," Cooper said and smiled.

Mary smiled back. Her heart flipped over in her chest. She thought that he was coming with bad news. Mary's intuition had been telling her all week something bad had happened, and something was terribly wrong with Joan.

To Mary's surprise, Sheriff Cooper kept walking down the street past her beauty parlor. He walked as if he was on a mission as he headed in the direction of the sheriff's office, two blocks down the street. She stood and watched him until Mary saw the postman walking down the street; he had just put mail in her mailbox. Her heart raced as she rushed over to the mailbox and pulled open the lid. Her hands shook with anticipation as she grabbed the letter lying there and tore it open. She quickly took it inside and sat down in her styling chair to read it. She wanted to read the letter before her next customer came. She began to read it and as she did, her heart beat hard in her chest. Ruth was letting her know that Joan was there with her. She suggested that Mary destroy the letter as soon as she was finished reading it, and then went on explaining what had happened and how Joan came to be in Floraville:

Helen, a widow lady who lived near the river, sometimes went for walks along the riverbank. Her husband died two years prior and walking and listening to the flow of the river soothed her weariness. She walked along the riverbank, the same path she always walked in the past two years. But, on this day as she looked down into river while she walked along, she noticed what looked like a dress caught up on some tree branches along the bank of the river. Helen thought that odd and looked closer. When Helen looked closer into the water, she saw that the dress was on a woman's body. And the woman was floating on her back with her face turned to the side. Helen could see her face and it was not blue or dead looking, not that she had seen that many dead people, only her husband when she found him dead next to her in bed one morning. So she knew what death looked like, it's a sight you don't easily forget.

Helen jumped into action seeing that the woman appeared to possibly be alive. She carefully stepped down the riverbank into the edge of the cold water. She had to creep out into the cold rushing water a bit further to be able to grab the branch the woman seems to be hung up on, in order to pull her closer. When she reached the woman she had to untangle the fishing line and limb that she was caught up in. Helen was careful to keep the woman's face above the flowing water while trying to keep her own balance as well, as the current wanted to take them both downstream. Helen worked as fast as she could but it seemed like it was taking her forever to untangle the woman. She worried that when she did get the woman untangled, that the current would pull her out of her hands and take her away. Finally, she got her free, and then carefully she managed to turn the woman's body enough so she could place her hands under her upper arms and hold her in place. She watched her footing so she wouldn't trip on limbs and brush on the edge of the river. She managed to drag the woman closer to the riverbank, and pull her on dry land, where she untangled more fishing line from around her. She rolled the woman on her stomach and pressed on her back, and pulled her shoulders back a bit to release the fishing line. She saw icy water run out the woman's mouth—pushes on her back must have helped revive the woman, because, the woman began coughing, then moaning, followed by more coughing. Helen held her own breath while waiting to see what was going to happen next. Suddenly, the woman began crying softly. Helen then helped her sit up.

"There, there, now," said Helen sounding concerned, "it will be all right. You are okay now," Helen thought the woman must have been walking on the path along the riverbank when she slipped and fell in and got tangled up in fishing line.

Joan managed to speak just above a whisper after a few minutes, and thanked the woman who rescued her. "Joan, my name is Joan," she said through tears. She was cold and shaking.

"My name is Helen. My god, what on earth happened to you?" asked Helen. She wondered how she would get her the rest of the way to her house. "Can you walk a bit if I hold you up?" asked Helen, "Can you put your arm around my shoulder?" Helen asked not knowing what else to do. She knew that she couldn't carry Joan all the way to her house.

"I can try to walk," whispered Joan in a weak but determined voice.

"Come on then, we'll just take our time," said Helen as she helped Joan by wrapping her arm around her waist and lifting. Joan managed to slowly walk toward Helen's house about a hundred yards away in plain view through the trees. Helen was determined to get Joan to her house.

She was so grateful she decided to go for a walk this day. *What a miracle to find this woman alive*, Helen thought. It was a tough slow struggle, but both women were determined to make it to Helen's house. Once there, Helen sat Joan on a kitchen chair and quickly lit a fire in the fireplace before she helped Joan get out her wet clothes. She saw that the woman had bruises all over her body and around her neck. She figured some of the bruises came from bumping against trees and limbs in the river, but she seriously wondered how she got the red marks and bruises around her neck. It looked like someone tried to strangle her. Helen filled the tub with hot water and helped Joan into it then got out clothes for her to wear. After Joan dried off and she helped dress her, Helen wrapped her in a blanket and had her sit on the sofa next to the fireplace. Helen then heated the leftover soup she had made for supper the evening before. The soup was good and hot and Joan sipped a little at a time. It seemed with each spoonful of nourishment that she was regaining her strength. As they sat bundled up near the fire, Joan explained to Helen what had happened, that her husband tried to kill her.

Helen was frightened for the woman and offered her place to her and said that she could stay there with her for as long as she needed to stay. Joan thanked her for her generosity but didn't want to stay more than a day or so before leaving town. She felt it would be dangerous for her to stay in Marysville, and she feared for Helen's safety too. Joan told Helen, Ruth's name and address in Floraville, that Mary had made her memorize. Joan wanted Helen to take her to the bus station, but Helen wouldn't hear of it and told her that she would drive her to Floraville herself.

Mary read the letter from Ruth with intent and enthusiasm. Ruth wrote in her letter, that she was happy to do whatever she could to help Joan and Helen was invited to stay, too. Helen had no one at home, so stayed on a few days as Ruth suggested.

Joan explained in detail what happened to her when they got to Ruth's house in Floraville. She told Ruth and Helen that she was not out for a leisurely walk that morning and slipped and fell into the river; but rather, her husband, Jess, strangled her unconscious and dumped her in the river. Ruth and Helen were appalled and swore they would help Joan in any way they could.

Ruth suggested Helen stay in Floraville. Helen liked the idea and said there was nothing for her in Marysville since her husband died. She would move to Floraville, but she needed something to do if she were to move there. "I'd like to start a small business," Helen mentioned. "I like to sew. I've been sewing all my life."

"Well, Floraville, just lost the owner of the dry goods store," explained Ruth, "so the business is there, ready for someone to take it over,"

"Well, that's perfect," smiled Helen, her eyes lit up with enthusiasm.

"How about we ask the property manager to show it to us tomorrow, before you return to Marysville?" Ruth asked.

It was a done deal! Helen liked the store size and the fact that it was right on Main Street. There was an upstairs apartment, which was perfect for her. It was all settled then, her husband had left her some money and she wanted a new start, and she liked Floraville from what she saw of it. She drove back to Marysville with a happy heart and promise for a new future. Ruth was going to help supply the store while Helen got her house in Marysville ready to sell. The ladies had bonded and were sorry to see Helen leave, but very happy to know that she was returning to stay.

Mary sat and cried after she read the letter from her sister. She was happy that Joan was safe; she also wished she could join them and move to Floraville, too. Ruth had written in her letter that she would love to have Mary there with them, away from Beau and Jess. Ruth said she could open a beauty parlor right there in Floraville, and she would help her get it set up, like she was doing for Helen's move there. Ruth ended her letter to Mary, by suggesting in future letters, that they use code words such as "flowers" or "garden," when referring to Joan. And warned Mary again to burn the letter immediately after reading it, because Joan's life was in danger—Jess had thought he killed her. Ruth added she was worried about Mary being there with Beau and Jess and to be very careful.

And there it was as clear as day, Jess thought he murdered Joan. His intent was to kill her. Mary felt an unknown panic she had never felt before. She immediately got out a box of matches and burned the letter and the envelope in the sink into ashes, and then washed the ashes down the drain. Gone, all traces of the letter were gone. Now she wondered, *Was it real? Did Jess really try to kill Joan?* Mary was in shock. She worked through her last customers of the day in a daze hoping her despair did not show on her face. When she was finished for the day and had time to think, she wondered if she really read that Jess threw Joan in the river. She only had a few minutes to think about what she learned, because it was time to fix super for Beau. He would be coming home from work soon. She hoped that he could not tell that she was hiding something. And she wondered if Jess ever mentioned Joan at all to

Beau. Did these brothers ever discuss their wives? Or did they only have booze and running hooch on their minds? She worried as she cooked dinner and set the table.

***

"How was your day?" asked Mary, when Beau sat down at the table.

"Oh you know, the usual. I worked on several cars today," he smiled. He was happy his work was good. The customers and this boss at the garage were pleased with his car repair skills. His boss told him that he was a natural mechanic and had real talent for trouble shooting mechanical problems. Beau shared his good news with Mary. Mary smiled and congratulated him; she was happy that he was happy. She wondered if that was why she was spared abuse, because Beau's days normally went well for him.

But what if they went bad, would he take it out on her, like Joan complained Jess took his frustrations out on her—even to the point where he tried to kill her. Mary was convinced that she was very intuitive, and that there was a reason why she had warned Joan. She knew it was just a matter of time before his temper would get worse and he would try to kill her. She was so glad that she gave Joan her sister's name and address in Floraville. She only hoped that Joan did not leave any trace that would lead Jess to her sister's house.

Chapter Six

The days passed and Beau and Jess had filled the jugs and loaded the truck and were out on the roads again making hooch deliveries. It was dark and it was raining very hard, as Beau and Jess headed down the county roads. Beau had been driving, but when they left the second-to-the-last stop at the customer's house. Jess jumped in to drive. He had just shared some hooch with the last customer and was feeling no pain. The old truck responded quickly to Beau's quick crank, which snapped back and nearly broke his arm. Beau had to jump out of the way, as Jess jumped behind the steering wheel preparing to drive and began heading out almost before Beau had a chance to run around to the side, jump in, get his leg in the door and shut it. The customer roared with laughter, as did Jess. Beau did not laugh. His arm hurt and he thought it wasn't funny. He knew better than to tell Jess to slow down though, much less ask him to pull over and let him drive. Trying to get

Jess to do something that he did not want to do was useless. They were lucky though, and made it to the last stop unscathed, and the truck was in one piece and still running. As they pulled up to the old farmhouse, they saw that the customer was sitting on the porch. As they got closer they heard him yelling at his wife.

"Old lady," the man called her and yelled curse words at her. He was a big guy with a big gut that stretched out the front of the ragged and faded overalls he wore. One suspender was hanging down and the other ready to fall off. He was dirty as was his ragged straw hat. He choked and coughed as he sucked on a corncob pipe, drawing in the tobacco smoke and puffing, trying to keep the tobacco lit. The air was heavy with the smell of burnt tobacco smoke and sour smelling sweaty clothes. The woman, his wife, was thin and looked tired. She had a bruise on the left side of her face, and Beau tried not to stare at it. But, Jess smirked at the sight of it. The large angry looking man walked clumsily down the porch steps. The wife remained out of the way and leaned against the porch railing. She looked too tired to stand up straight on her own. As the big man came closer to the truck, he smirked and laughed with the men.

"Men folk just got to whip them into shape once in a while," the big round man said, " and let them know who is boss." The man grunted and then spit his chewed up tobacco wad on the ground at Beau's feet.

"Isn't that the truth," laughed Jess and slapped the guy's back in agreement.

"Yep, we men folk have to keep our women folk in line," the big guy said, then chuckled.

Beau did not say anything as he turned and looked at the woman. She seemed to be in a daze, staring into space, with a faraway look in her eyes as if her body was searching for her mind. Beau felt bad for her, but there was nothing he could do. He reached into the back of the truck and dug two jugs of hooch from the straw. The big man smiled, showing three yellow teeth, when he saw the jugs. He knew better than to take the jugs before paying. He paid Jess, then took the two jugs from Beau.

With one in either of his big claw like hands, he lifted them high to check the weight to make sure they felt full to the top. He sat one of the jugs down on the ground, while he pulled out the cork and took a big swig from the other jug. He laughed then coughed, then smiled. He then did the same with the second jug, lifting it high and then pulling the cork and taking a big swig. Yeah, he was satisfied, and it was time for the brothers to go. Beau jumped in behind the steering wheel before Jess had a chance. Jess grumbled, as he turned the crank then slide into the passenger seat and shut the door. As Beau pulled out of the yard, he turned to look back just as the man slapped the woman in the face again, so hard it knocked her off the side of the porch onto the ground. Beau wanted to stop and he pushed and pulled on the brakes. Jess saw it too, but yelled at Beau to mind his own business.

"Women need to be taken down a few notches from time to time, to let them know who's boss," declared Jess. "I know, I had to do that with my old lady." Jess bragged and let out an evil laugh. And then Jess thought he better shut up, and so he did.

"Just how is Joan?" Beau suddenly heard himself asking Jess. "You haven't mentioned her lately." Many a time Beau wondered about Joan, but was afraid to ask.

"Oh yeah, she's been behaving all right," was all that Jess was willing to share. He had had enough booze so even he was afraid that he might say too much. But he couldn't help it. He just had to go on.

"That bitch ran off with that salesman," said Jess. He even had himself believing that was what actually happened

"That sure doesn't seem like Joan," Beau commented, but Jess didn't want to hear any of it.

"Oh, so what." Jess laughed. "What if I just threw her in the river, she is easy enough to replace." Jess laughed a loud wicked laugh. Beau did not like what he heard.

By then they were at the next stop, on the route of deliveries, and the talk of wives was over. That sale went off without a hitch and so they went on to the next stop. The whole day and next day went well for them. They were lucky, there were no problems with customers or competitors, and no sheriff deputies got in their way, either.

Most delivery trips were about the same. Beau and

Jess had to drive all night and part of the next day to complete all of their deliveries without causing suspicion at their work places. As long as the work got done their bosses at the gas station garage and feed store did not care.

Their pappy's reputation of having an evil temper, preceded them, and everyone thought them to be the same, so never wanted to rile their feathers. It wasn't worth getting shot. As it was, their pappy only got into two street fights, where he killed men, he said was in self-defense. One man had cheated him at cards and pappy challenged him. Pappy was just a faster draw. The story got exaggerated through the years and people were easily scared. Folks stepped aside and gave the bothers all the leeway they wanted. Particularly their bosses, who were well aware of the silent volcano that lay deep within, and was likely to erupt without a warning, so they allowed them to choose the hours they were willing to work, as long as the work got done in a timely fashion.

***

Like most evenings at home, conversation was casual as Beau and Mary ate supper. Beau did most of the talking that Friday evening. He had just bought fresh supplies, and he was planning on going to the cabin for the weekend to distill hooch. He was always careful to pick up grain and supplies for making booze at various places on his way back from his deliveries up north, to not lead to suspicions by local authorities. Sometimes he would trade jugs of booze for the grain supplies that he needed from the farmers. He was happy, successful, and smart and he knew it.

Beau never spoke of Jess much, and Mary did not ever dare ask him about Jess. She never did before the incident with Joan, so why start now. She just had to wonder if Beau knew about Joan or not. But, Mary wondered, wouldn't it seem odd if she didn't mention Joan. She tried to remember, did she ever talk about Joan? Did she ever tell Beau that Joan came into the beauty parlor to get her hair done? Beau never asked about such things, so maybe she didn't. She was beginning to second guess herself. She was getting nervous. She reminded herself to just act natural like she always did. Beau usually did all the talking, so let him talk. Tomorrow he would be gone at the cabin all weekend and then probably the next weekend make a hooch run to near Springfield with Jess. But then something happened—Beau brought up Jess, out of the blue, as Mary was gathering up the dishes to place in the kitchen sink.

"Jess said Joan left him," said Beau sounding very serious, "Have you seen her?" Beau asked rather sternly. He sounded as if Joan suddenly went crazy and up and left her husband. Mary thought he also sounded like he was warning her, not to get any crazy ideas like Joan, and up and leave him. This made Mary very nervous.

"I've wondered where she has been," answered

Mary speaking carefully and trying not to sound too little concerned or too overly concerned.

"She hasn't come to see you, then?" asked Beau looking at her oddly, as if she was holding out on him.

"I haven't seen her," Mary said, "I wondered where she has been."

"Well, Jess said she up and left him. Jess said he thought she probably took off with that broom, household and cleaning products salesman that always comes to town. Jess said he hasn't seen either of them lately."

"Oh my, I had no idea," Mary said. "My, no wonder I haven't seen her." Mary was surprised all right; she was surprised at the crazy excuse Jess gave Beau for Joan's disappearance.

Beau left it at that and said he was going to bed. He would be getting up probably at daybreak then would head up to the cabin. Mary quietly washed the dishes, then slipped into bed not to disturb Beau's sleep. She could not sleep and stared at the ceiling, as he laid there next to her in a sound sleep. She laid there in deep thought, *What a lame excuse, saying Joan ran off with a broom salesman. What happens when the broom salesman comes back into town? Will Jess take care of him too like he did Joan in order to stop him before he claims he doesn't know Joan and she is not with him.*

Mary suspected Beau was the only one he told that Joan ran off with the salesman. She was sure that Jess never visited the dry goods store, and that the storeowner, Marge, never met Joan's husband, Jess. Oh,

Mary was well aware there was lots of gossip in a small town like Marysville. She heard firsthand how they gossiped when several ladies were in the beauty parlor at the same time. They gossiped all right, but most of the time, Mary noticed, the women just complained about their husbands, children, in-laws and neighbors. So Mary figured that not much time was left over to even think about poor quiet Joan.

***

Mary was glad to be busy with her beauty parlor work on Saturday, it was Sundays that were the loneliest, but still she was glad that Beau was gone. Mary could not get Joan and Ruth off her mind the entire weekend. She kept busy and worked in the yard on Sunday afternoon, picking up fallen tree branches and raking leaves. She was working close to the sidewalk near the house, when a tall shadow figure of a man formed on the ground in front of her from behind. The sudden sight of it overshadowing her in the mid-afternoon sun frightened her. She turned sharply to see who it was, and her heart suddenly sank, it was Jess.

"Hey doll, how you doing?" asked Jess. He had been drinking, of course, and spoke in a wickedly cheerful voice.

"Oh Jess, I didn't see you there," exclaimed Mary, "what brings you this way?" Mary showed a fake smile as she tried to sound relaxed and it took every effort she could muster. She didn't like him being there, and the way he sneaked up on her gave her the creeps. "Beau is not home," Mary, announced, before Jess could mutter another word. She wanted him to leave. She tried to sound casual but it was very hard to do when her insides were shaking.

"Oh, I didn't come by to see Beau, honey," Jess replied, "I come by to see you." He smiled showing uneven yellow teeth only slightly hidden behind a ragged beard.

Mary did not know what to say. When she was just about to faint or throw up, she heard Beau's voice.

"There you are!" Beau said. "Come on, Jess. Let's get going and make some deliveries yet today, before it gets too late," urged Beau. Jess only grunted and turned to join Beau.

"The yard looks nice, Mary," Beau said and he smiled as he turned to follow Jess out of the yard. He was always glad to see Mary working around the house. "Idle hands are the devil's workshop," he always said.

"The yard looks nice, Mary," mocked Jess, in a way that said he really didn't want to leave just yet but wanted to keep on talking to her. As they walked away Mary breathed a sigh of relief and went into the house. She locked the door and wished she were in Floraville with her sister.

***

They headed out of town, with Beau driving the old pick-up. He drove slowly down the street not to attract attention. They made a point to leave town at different times and took different routes. They were visiting hunting and fishing buddies and had their guns and fishing equipment with them, just in case the law stopped them and they were asked what they were up to. The law didn't have to know those buddies were hooch customers. The hooch jugs were kept well hidden, stuffed between straw bales in the back of the truck. Beau and Jess both knew that their hooch customers would not call the sheriff, certainly not since they were willingly buying illegal alcohol. Illegal hooch running was fairly easy; still, there were dangers in anything profitable. Jess and Beau had learned early on, that the hooch business was risky, but they thrived on danger and competition. The county roads were unsafe at night with reckless drivers on bad roads, and with hooch dealers trying to sell their booze supply before the competition got to their customers, but that was just the danger that went with the occupation and they thrived on it.

Chapter Seven

Mary kept busy in the beauty parlor styling ladies' hair. It had been over a week since she heard from her sister, Ruth, and she was feeling sad. So as soon as she saw the postman walk away from the mailbox, she hurried out front to the street and checked inside the mailbox. She had a feeling she was going to hear from her sister that day and she did. Mary ran inside with the letter and tore the envelope open as she sat down in her styling chair to read it.

Her sister wrote that she had been working in the garden and it was looking good and came in handy for her in the pastry shop. Mary was glad to hear all was well and quickly burned the letter and the envelope without a return address on it. She did not want any signs of communication left behind for Jess, Beau, or anyone else to see. She thought about the postman, George, and how people said he liked to read postcards and looked over people's mail and knew their business that way.

Mary was worried about that talk and gossip regarding Joan and Jess. She was sick with worry most of the time lately, and it made her sick to her stomach because of it. If something like that could happen to Joan, it could happen to any woman, and Mary was afraid. Oh she respected her husband Beau all right; that is, if you confuse the meaning of respect with fear. She made sure to walk the line and do nothing to make him angry.

Beau wanted kids. Mary was not happy about this yet performed her wifely duties. No wonder she had miscarriages she thought, she was nothing but a bundle of nerves. The doctor just suggested they keep on trying, that one day it may take. Mary really did not want kids. Oh she knew that if she had a child she would love it, be it a boy or girl. But, she wasn't sure that she wanted to bring up a child in this unsettled dangerous environment of hooch runners, thieves and attempted murderers—namely Jess. Mary thought it was just a matter of time before Beau and Jess ran into the law, doing the unlawful and end up in jail or worse, dead. What kind of legacy would that be for a son or daughter? And then the worst did happen.

***

It was late in the day. Mary had just finished with her last customer, and was straightening up her beauty parlor, when she saw the postman pass by her window. She ran out to check the mailbox. She was sorry to find that there was no letter from Ruth. She was deep in thought as she walked back to the porch, grabbed the broom and began sweeping the sidewalk and steps leading up to the beauty parlor door. A bad feeling came over her, as if the air suddenly was filled with an evil energy. She looked up and saw Jess. He appeared out of nowhere, and of course he was drunk.

"How you doing today, pretty lady?" He swooned, smiling, smelling of booze, and standing much too close. *Why was he hanging around her?* she wondered. How she prayed Beau would show up. No way was she going to let him inside.

"Hi, Jess. How are you today?" She tried to sound cheerful, hoping that if she were reasonably kind to him, he would just say hello, then be on his way. She certainly did not want to be rude and set him off in a rant.

"Hi, I could be a lot better, pretty lady," Jess smiled as he looked Mary up and down from head to foot. He stopped short, when he saw they had company.

"Oh hi, Sheriff Cooper," Mary said. She was never so glad to see anyone in her whole life.

"Hello, Mary," smiled Sheriff Cooper tipping the brim of his service hat, in greeting.

"This man bothering you?" Sheriff Cooper asked it in a kind of kidding way, but in a way to let Mary know that he meant what he said, and was there to protect her. Sheriff Cooper knew Jess was a drunk. He had to get the booze from somewhere so either he was buying it or he was distilling it for himself. Cooper figured it was the latter. Lots of people were doing that, and the law didn't mess with the small time distillers as long as they only sold small quantities.

"I was just checking on the lady, Sheriff," said Jess with a smirk.

"Well, I'm here now, by the way, where is, Beau?" The sheriff asked. Jess only made a big smile that showed his crooked yellow teeth.

"And where is your wife, Jess?" Cooper asked with an accusing sneer in his voice.

"You know she done run off," said Jess, sounding all down and out. "She done ran off with a salesman, I tell you." Jess said trying to sound like he was about to cry.

"What salesman did she run off with then, Jess?" Sheriff Cooper asked. "I know you were punching her around. I've seen the bruises." Sheriff Cooper knew Jess only too well and through the years it seemed he only got worse.

"What are you accusing me of sheriff?" Jess was getting hot under the collar. Mary was afraid they might get into a fist fight. But then it looked like Jess was backing down. Mary was sure that this wasn't the end of it. Jess would be back again to bother her, and she knew it.

"Go on home now Jess, I don't want to see you hanging around here unless Beau is home," demanded Sheriff Cooper. Mary kept quiet. She wanted to go inside and hide. Finally, Sheriff Cooper nodded in her direction, as if to tell her to get inside now. She took the broom in with her, shut the door and locked it. She shook as she stood behind the locked door. The two men walked away from her beauty parlor door, each going in the opposite direction. *Where was Beau?* Mary wondered.

Beau finally came home from working at the garage. He said his boss wanted him to finish a job while the customer waited. The customer was a salesman and needed his car so he waited while Beau replaced the brake line. Beau said the break line usually wears through from the rain, mud and grim on the road. But it actually looked like this brake line was cut almost in half. Beau got the line repaired and the salesman went on his way, and Beau ended his workday and went home. Mary listened to Beau as he talked about his day, as she stood at the stove and cooked potatoes and fried ham for supper. He was more talkative than usual, as if he was talking out loud to himself, retracing the steps of his day.

"The brake line appeared to be cut," Beau said, sounding serious, "which seemed odd to me." He scratched his head trying to figure out how that happened.

Of course, he was thinking mechanically, not maliciously, and deliberately cutting a brake line would never occur to Beau like it would to Jess, thought Mary.

"The line was not worn or torn, but cut," said Beau as if he couldn't get over that. "Oh, well," he said, as Mary placed dishes of food on the table, and he turned in his chair then to face his plate and picked up the folk, ready to dig in, he was hungry.

Mary heard every word he said and understood what it meant. And Beau meant it looked like someone cut the brake line so the salesman would have no brakes and then wreck the car. She wondered if it was the broom salesman Jess accused his wife of running off with. Of course Mary knew better. But, had Jess convinced himself that Joan did in fact run off with the salesman? She knew, her sister knew and Helen, the woman, who pulled Joan out of the river, knew that Joan did not run off with a salesman. Jess was spewing rumors about town to explain the disappearance of Joan. The sad part was the salesman had no clue he was being used to take the blame for Joan's disappearance.

Mary kept her mouth shut and did not say anything to Beau. Blood was thicker than water are so the saying goes, and Joan thought if it came right down to it, if their backs were against the wall, Beau would hold up for his brother, just as she would hold up for her sister.

They finished supper in silence, Beau only speaking to tell Mary that the supper was very good. He remained in deep thought as he ate. And while he ate, he remembered that Jess said a salesman done run off with his wife. This being southern Illinois, they were considered "out in the sticks," and not that many salesmen passed through this area. Beau wondered if he should tell the sheriff about the cut brake line, so the sheriff could keep an eye on the salesman. Beau figured whoever cut the brake line, could just as easily cut it again. He decided against saying anything to the sheriff, for fear his brother may be involved. Seemed Jess took after their daddy and had a mean streak running down his backbone. Beau also decided he was not going to mention anything to Jess about fixing the salesman's brake line. Beau thought. The salesman won't be back for another month and maybe by then Joan will turn up again.

***

It was getting hard for Mary to concentrate on what her customers told her they wanted her to do. She almost cut a woman's hair too short; so it was a good thing the woman spoke up. Mary knew that she had to get a grip on things. Her intuition was telling her that something was about to happen. Something was about to blow. She could feel it in the air, but it wasn't going to be the weather that stirred up a big fuss, it was going to be Jess. She could feel the bad energy that radiated from him already. She could feel it in her bones whenever Jess came around.

Mary was finished for the day and while putting the "closed" sign in the window, Mary saw Sheriff Cooper near the beauty parlor door. Should she tell him what she knew? No, she thought, it wasn't time yet. Besides it was Jess's word against hers. No one would take a woman's word over a man's word. Jess would deny everything. There was no proof anything had happened and that there was an attempt on Joan's life. Mary was afraid of what Jess could do. She knew that he would deny it, and claim Joan was going crazy and have her institutionalized. It only took a man's word or a bribed doctor to have someone committed.

Mary just knew Jess would send Joan up to Alton, to the insane asylum, and have her committed for a very long time, if not forever. Mary had to be careful what she said, because she could end up there in the insane asylum herself. She heard the gossiping ladies in her beauty parlor say many men did that when they got tired of their wives and wanted to get rid of them. The Catholic Church said divorce was wrong, and a cause for excommunication. But, a husband could just say the wife was insane and have her put away some place.

Jess had thought of sending Joan to the nut house, but then his temper got in the way. Joan got on his drunken nerves. Her loud shrill voice touched his last nerve and he had to shut her up in a hurry. He reacted in impulsive anger, and lost sense of what he was doing for a moment. And when he came back around again to reality, he found his hands around her neck—choking her hard. It gave him great pleasure to see her squirm, then slump and drop to the floor. The high point of his rage came when he knocked her on side of the head with the heavy iron skillet. Joan was gone and with her out of the way, and Jess wanted Mary.

He had always wanted Mary, but then Beau got in the way. His younger brother always wanted everything he had. He had Mary first, before Beau had enough nerve to steal her away. He had never forgiven Beau for that, and he was going to get Mary back, one way or the other. He was tired of keeping quiet about it. No way, did Beau know. Beau thought everything was just fine when shortly after Beau married Mary, Jess married Joan. But the real truth was Jess married Joan out of spite. Beau took his girl, and he wasn't going to be without one and be all alone. Oh, Joan was fine enough, for a while that is, until he grew tired of her. Jess did not love Joan, so everything she did got on his nerves and reminded him that Mary would not have gotten on his nerves, everything she would have been beautiful and perfect.

Mary would have known what he liked. She would know how he liked his eggs, how he liked his ham fried, coated with a little butter and flour, then fried in lard. Mary would have remembered how strong he liked his coffee in the morning. He got angry just thinking about what he did not have. He was glad Joan was gone. He would find a way now to get Beau out of the way so he could have Mary back for himself. He just had to wait until the time was right, but was sure that it would happen.

***

Mary received another letter from her sister saying the garden and the flowers were healthy and growing. Her sister Ruth's pastry shop was doing well. Writing that the garden was healthy and growing was a way of saying that everything was well. That Joan was there to help her in her pastry shop. Mary wept when she read the letter. She wished that she could be there with them. When she finished reading it, she held it close to her heart just for a second. Then hurriedly got out of the matches and burned it in the sink just like she had burned all the other letters she had received for the past year and a half. She wiped her tears before she unlocked the beauty parlor door to receive her first morning customer.

At least she had this job, she thought, and could save money for her escape from Marysville. And this was a reality that she promised herself. It was her dream of escape that kept her going from day to day. Beau went to work at the gas station garage every day and on weekends to the cabin on the mountain to distill hooch. It was time for another weekend run up north with a truck load of booze. One day was like another for her in Marysville.

***

Jess and Beau filled the truck with jugs and were on their way out of town but stopped by Mary's beauty parlor. Mary saw them pull up and met Beau in the kitchen to give him sandwiches and say good-bye. Jess stayed in the truck, and Mary was glad that he did. Jess had not been bothering her lately and she was grateful for that.

"We're heading out to get an earlier start than usual, we want to be back in time to go to work on Monday morning," Beau said as he headed out the door. Mary did not know much about the hooch running business, but she did know that Beau and Jess liked to leave at different times of the day and take different routes so they wouldn't stir up suspicion or run into other bootleggers trying to steal their territory.

There were enough customers for all the bootleggers in the counties all the way to Springfield. The more money they made the bigger the distillery businesses became. Many bootleggers made enough to buy bigger trucks so they could haul more hooch in one trip and have more customers. Beau and Jess had big dreams too, and they were making enough money where they thought another distillery in the cellar would bring them more cash, and then they would buy a bigger truck. They felt they were getting rich, but of course along with more money comes more greed. Soon Jess did not want to share the money with Beau.

Down deep in his gut, Jess hated Beau. He always thought their pappy liked Beau best. He was the oldest, Pappy Hank should have liked him more, given him more. Pappy Hank had always said if anything happened to him, Beau gets the house, Beau gets the cabin. Beau gets this, Beau gets that. Jess was sick of it. Jess's memories of his pappy favoring Beau was eating him up. The drunken stupors he was in most of the time didn't help either. He was becoming paranoid. He thought Beau was out to get him, so he had to get him first.

Beau noticed a change in Jess. It was getting harder

and harder to work in the close quarters of the cellar distillery with Jess. Jess was bossy and demanding and crabby all the time. Beau just wanted to get the hooch made and sell it. The road trips were tough. Jess was drunk but he always wanted to drive—nearly drove off the road several times on their last run and almost killed them both. And Jess was always ready to argue price with the customer, sometimes almost getting in to knock down drag out fist fights. Beau told him that they may start losing customers because of the way he acted, but Jess didn't care. He just swore that he was right and everybody else was wrong.

Jess was beginning to hate his brother Beau even more because little brother thought he was so smart, telling him how to act and all. The alcohol quantities that he consumed were making him crazy in the head and sick in the gut and downright mad.

Chapter Eight

It was Sunday evening, late. Beau was riding shotgun and Jess was driving like a crazy man. They had sold the last jug of liquor just south of Springfield and were heading back to Marysville. They drove the back roads weaving in and out of curves and flying up and down hills through the woods. Suddenly there was a deer standing in the middle of the road as they crested a steep hill. Beau yelled out and Jess swerved to the right to miss the deer. Jess missed the deer all right, but as he jerked the steering wheel and swerved right, then left again, Beau's door flew open and he flew out of the truck and tumbled into darkness. As he hit the ground, he tumbled and rolled but managed to keep a grip on to the rifle he had been holding. He slid down a steep embankment and landed unconscious near the edge of a lake.

Jess was drinking from a jug while he drove and did not even notice that Beau had been thrown from the truck. He just concentrated on watching the road as best he could. The headlights were dim and he had to strain to see where he was going but it did not slow him down. When the jug was empty, he turned to hand it to Beau—he was astonished to see Beau was not sitting there. The passenger side door had swung shut again at the next curve after Beau had been thrown out so it seemed as if Beau just disappeared into thin air. Jess's eyes grew large as he strained to see Beau. He almost ran off the road and hit a tree, but he swung back the other way just in time. The steering wheel had jerked in his hands, almost busting his fingers. He hurt like hell and almost felt sober, as if that was even possible. Jess had not been sober in months. His preferred state as of late was a state of intoxication.

Where was Beau? Did he leave him back at the last stop? He thought that he was going absolutely crazy. And then he thought maybe the booze was poisoned somehow, and poisoned his brain and drove him nuts. He did not know where to begin to look for Beau. And so he drove the rest of the way home in a stupor, bouncing in his seat on the gut jarring rutted roads, crying and laughing at the same time feeling like a crazy man.

He wanted to drive straight through the night to Marysville. But, when it was close to dawn, he heard the last half gallon or so sloshing around in the gas tank. He thought he better get gas, because he would never make it to Marysville on what little he had left. So he drove into Floraville for gas and something to eat.

It was dawn and the sun was just coming up. It looked like the town was just waking up. He was sleepy and had a horrible headache. Black coffee, he needed black coffee. He really wanted booze. While the truck was filling up with gas at the gasoline station, Jess rooted around under the straw in the bed of the truck and searched for a forgotten jug of hooch. He rooted around until he found one. Eureka! His spirits were lifted. He held on to the jug and quickly climbed into the cab of the truck. When he thought no one was looking he lifted the jug and took a huge swig of the precious liquid that kept his brain working and his body moving.

The truck was filled up with gas, and Jess needed to fill his stomach. There was no further thought of Beau, where he was, or if he was alive. Out of sight, was out of mind as far as Jess was concerned. Jess was hungry. He looked in the pastry shop on Main Street and thought about sitting at the counter for coffee and some coffee cake. But that sounded too sweet and the Breakfast Diner was right there, so he headed to it instead. As he walked closer he could smell bacon frying. Man was he hungry, and so he staggered in and sat down clumsily on a stool at the counter. If there had been a sheriff there, he would have been questioned because he smelled of straight up booze. It was on his breath and spilled on his dirty bid overalls.

Without asking the waitress behind the counter set a full cup of strong black coffee in the front of him. He didn't bother looking at the big chalkboard menu on

the wall behind the counter, just said what he wanted —
lots of bacon and eggs. The waitress was pleasant
enough. She knew from experience how to handle his
kind. She thought that the drunken bum probably did
not have any money, but she would serve him anyway,
just to feed him and get him out of there as quickly as
she could. As it was no one sat within six feet of him,
because of the stink.

Jess sat waiting as patiently as he could for his
breakfast. The diner was busy that morning. He was
just going to have a wait. The waitress was moving as
fast as she could. No one wanted to see him out of there
more than she did. To confront an unlikely sort such
as he and try to turn him away only caused more grief
than it was worth.

As he sat there, looking around, Jess casually
turned around and looked out the diner window that
faced Main Street. A woman walked by, an attractive
woman Jess thought, and he thought that she looked
familiar. The woman was smiling and walked with
determination. There was something about her. Jess
took a sip of the second cup of freshly poured coffee
placed in front of him. He could not help but stare at the
woman walking past the window. She was gone now,
past the window and out of sight. It took Jess a few
minutes but suddenly in all his brainless drunkenness
realized who the woman had reminded him of — Joan.
Of course, Joan. She was the spitting imagine of Joan.
Joan, whose body he had tied in fishing line to a big
branch and pushed her into the fast flowing river. Pain

in the ass, Joan! The woman who passed by the diner's window could have been her twin.

Jess's messed up brain began playing tricks on him. What if it was Joan? Oh my god. He thought that he was going nuts. First Beau disappears than Joan reappears. Holy shit. Jess choked down the bacon and eggs, threw down some money, and got the hell out of there. Back to the safety of his truck and his jug, he quickly drove out of Floraville and headed to Marysville. Crying and laughing as he drove. He didn't know which way was up, he just drove.

As he drove on and had time to settle down, he had to think of something to tell Mary. He was driving Beau's truck, without Beau. He lost Beau! Seems, Mary was the only sane thing in his life now. Dear Mary. Mary would welcome him with open arms. Just as Beau was out of sight, out of mind, Jess thought that Mary would have the same reaction and run to Jess with open arms when she saw him. He laughed. He was happy. His Mary was waiting for him.

Chapter Nine

Joan smiled as she opened the door to the pastry shop. She was ready to join Ruth behind the counter serving customers. For some reason, Joan had an odd feeling this morning as she walked past the window of the Breakfast Diner. She had one of those feelings you get when someone is staring at you from across the way. She couldn't shake the feeling, and it haunted her as she waited on customers and put dough in the oven to bake. She served a variety of sweet smelling pastries, which made Ruth's shop so famous. While waiting to open the oven door, Joan watched Ruth behind the counter chatting with a customer.

Joan had come to love Ruth who had so graciously taken her in to live with her. She loved Helen, too. Joan had just stopped by to deliver pastry to Helen. Helen had moved to Floraville after she sold her house in Marysville and opened the sewing shop and a dry goods store. She lived in the apartment above the store and was very happy there. The dry goods store was located on the corner of Main Street and Fifth Street just two blocks from the pastry shop. Life was good in Floraville for Helen just as it was good there for Joan.

Since Joan had begun a new life in Floraville she had practically forgotten all about Jess, and how he had beaten and choked her and knocked her unconscious with a skillet, and then he threw her in the river. She felt nothing for him. She did not want to waste her energy and time lowering herself to his level to even hate him. It wasn't worth it. She was grateful for her new beginning in life — her rebirth of a second chance. She was free and she was happy, and she felt loved.

Chapter Ten

The first stop Jess wanted to make when he was back home in Marysville was Beau and Mary's place. He wanted to see if Beau was there. What would he tell Mary if he wasn't there and she asked where he was? Jess decided he was going to tell Mary he thought Beau was with her, that Beau got a ride back home with another guy because Jess wanted to stop in Floraville for a while, and Beau wanted to get home to Mary. So Jess rehearsed what he was going to say.

"Hello, Mary," Jess said rather sweetly he thought when he entered the door to her beauty parlor. The two women there just stared at the filthy person who staggered in the door. They thought for sure he was a bum off the street who came into the beauty parlor by mistake. Mary was at the shampoo bowl scrubbing a woman's head and about passed out at the horrid sight she saw when she looked up and saw him coming through the door. She cursed herself for not keeping the damn door locked—which she realized of course, was rather hard to do when she depended on walk-in customers to fill her day. But nonetheless, she still wished she had locked the door. People could knock, after all.

"What?" Mary asked.

"Is Beau here?" Jess asked slurring his words and bumping into the wall almost knocking over the hall tree filled with coats. It was a wonder, Mary thought, he managed to catch it as well as he did before it tumbled over, coats and all.

"Beau went with you," Mary said. She was scared and now puzzled.

"He did, but then he ran into a buddy and got a ride back to town with him," Jess smiled showing yellow teeth that just about turned Mary's stomach. The sight of him was appalling.

"Well, Beau is not here. I have not heard from him nor seen him," Mary answered Jess rather sternly. She felt a little braver with two other women in the room as witnesses. In the past, Mary had more faith in Jess and thought he would not do something stupid, but she was changing her mind, because it appeared Jess was in a continuous drunken state as of late, much worse than he had ever been.

And it was becoming the norm for him the past few months. Ever since Joan disappeared Mary thought Jess has been acting weird. Served him right, she thought. He was being self-destructive and she was glad to see it. The sooner he fell, the better, she thought.

Jess looked around the room filled with ladies. He wasn't sure what to do. He wanted to sweet talk Mary, but not in the front of these women. Just then Sheriff Cooper popped his head in the door to check on Mary, and she was so glad he did. Usually the sheriff got on her nerves, but today she was glad to see him. She was nervous around drunken Jess. Mary had the funny feeling that Sheriff Cooper was following Jess around town, and she was glad. It just seemed that when Jess showed up, Sheriff Cooper wasn't far behind.

"How you doing ma'am?" asked Cooper. "Just thought I'd come by and check on you," he said as he smiled and tipped his hat. He placed his hand on his revolver as he turned and looked at Jess. *How could Jess smell of alcohol and be drunk all the time if the stuff was illegal and not allowed to be sold? Jess must have alcohol stocked up somewhere that he's drinking,* thought Sheriff Cooper. He was going to confront Jess about it, but then thought the better of it with the ladies sitting right there and Mary trying to work. So Cooper gave up the idea and thought he'd check on that with Jess at a later date.

Cooper watched as Jess staggered back out the door and toward the truck, managed to crank it and it started right up. Slowly he climbed in and headed toward his house, where he flopped on the sofa and fell fast asleep.

Chapter Eleven

Beau regained consciousness and discovered he was lying at the bottom of a hillside. It was dark and he did not know where he was. The only thing that he remembered was that when Jess sped around the curve he was thrown against the door, and it flew open and he flew out of the truck and tumbled and rolled down a long steep hillside. He remembered holding on to the rifle as he fell out of the truck. He had lay there for a moment and looked up at the full moon and wondered where he was. The sky was clear and the stars were bright and felt so close, he thought he could reach up and touch them. The tree frogs chirped noisily as did the bull frogs in the water nearby. He could hear flopping sounds and water splashing. It was dark and he couldn't see the lake very well, but the water sounded deep and refreshing, and he was very thirsty.

His head hurt, his whole body ached. He was afraid

to move. He did not know the extent of his injuries and tried to assess the damage as he lay there, first moving his arms, then his legs, then lifting his head up. He hurt but nothing felt broken. All seemed to be okay. He touched his forehead and it felt wet, then his hand felt wet. In the moonlight he saw a small spot on blood on his hand. So he wasn't bleeding that bad, just a scratch. He tried to sit up then, and that went okay. He felt dirty and scratched up pretty bad.

Turning away from the lake, he looked up and could not believe he missed all those trees and had found the only clear path to roll all the way down to the lake. It had to be twenty yards or more—he was never good at judging distance. And if a truck or car went by he could not tell because the road was too far above him. There probably wouldn't be anybody driving by during the night anyway. He wondered what time it was and how long he had been lying there unconscious. Should he try to climb back up the hill? He looked around for the rifle, I least he would have that if he could find it. He ached and he was cold and he was tired. He thought he could just lay there till dawn.

And then through the trees he saw the light of dawn rising on the horizon. So that's east, he thought. Even if he did get up and climb back up the hill, did he know which way to walk. He felt turned around. He thought, *Well, if the sun is coming up in the east, when I get up to the top of the hill I should turn left then and walk that way.* He felt dizzy and lay back down on the tall grass that surrounded him. It was peaceful and quiet, so he lay there for a minute pondering his next move. First, he should look for the rifle.

He heard the gentle sound of a cow mooing in a distance. Oh, and a rooster crowed at the first light of day. There had to be a farm nearby. He was hungry, and wondered if he could even walk straight once he did manage to get up. He got on his knees then looked up the steep hill and there not far up above his head, was the rifle wedged between several small trees trunks. He hung onto branches and managed to crawl a few feet, until he was able to reach the rifle and wiggle until he pulled it loose. It slid the rest of the way down the hill to where he landed. What an awful feeling it was to fly out that truck not knowing what he was going to hit, or where he was going to land. As it was, he must have hit his head on a tree trunk, and knocked himself out. He had to have been lying there for hours, because he thought they have been passing through that area maybe around nine or ten at night, when he flew out.

And where in the hell was Jess? If Jess would not have been driving like just an idiot he would not have flown out of the damn truck. For all he knew, Jess may have wrecked the truck and Jess could be somewhere nearby. Beau had no idea. It was getting lighter now and he could see his surroundings better. He saw a barn in the distance and there was a grassy pasture on the other side of the lake. He thought he could walk around the lake and through the pasture to the farm. Who knows, maybe he would find Jess there looking for him. He hurt all over, but started to walk in the direction of the barn. It had to be a good mile or so to walk. He had no idea.

It took him a while. He had to sit and rest now and then. It was quiet and peaceful, and he did a lot of thinking as he walked. He thought about giving up the hooch business. He didn't really need all the excitement and danger of it all. He had a job at the filling station, pumping gas and working on the cars and trucks that came in for repair. So why did he need to follow in his old pappy's footsteps anyway? The distillery had been his pappy's idea. Then Jess wanted to take it over, but the booze was over taking Jess.

It took Beau a while, but he made the trek to the farm place. He saw light in the window. Then heard a dog bark. Before he could get to the front porch steps the door opened and a man holding a rifle stood there. Beau made sure that he carried his rifle in one hand and had the barrow pointed at the ground so he wouldn't look threatening.

"Good morning. Don't mean to disturb you. I lost my way and fell back yonder. Was wandering around lost, and then saw your farm," Beau said sounding weak and looking a wreck.

"Oh. You look like a decent sort of fellow. A little banged up, maybe, but come on in and get some coffee," the man kindly offered with a grin, holding the door open for Beau. "My name is Frank."

"Beau. The name is Beau," he managed to say. He hurt walking up the three steps to the porch and held onto the hand rail. Each step hurt his legs and back.

"Looks like you took a real tumble," said Frank sounding sympathetically.

"Sure did," said Beau as he pressed his hand to his aching back. He propped his rifle against the porch railing, before he walked into the house.

The farmer's dog lay down at his feet, as he sat at the kitchen table and sipped the hot coffee Frank poured and set in front of him. Beau was grateful. He began to relax and looked around at his surroundings. The place looked like it had a woman's touch with nice curtains and pictures on the wall. But, he did not see anyone else there. Frank saw him looking around.

"My wife went to our son's place down the road. His wife just had a new baby and Martha is helping out," Frank said proudly. He was happy and proud of his farm and family and all the hard work they had put into it to keep it going. He and his son did all the planting and harvesting, milking the cows and raising the pigs and chickens. Martha tended to the house and garden. Their cellar was well stocked for winter. He offered ham and eggs to Beau.

"Oh, I hate to put you out, but I sure am hungry," said Beau beginning to salivate at the thought of eating ham and eggs. "I can't remember the last time I ate," admitted Beau.

He knew Frank thought he was a bum. One of those guys who can't find work and who walked along the roads hitch-hiking or walked down the train tracks every now and then and stop and ask for a sandwich and water from the well. Frank did not mind helping him out.

And Beau did not mind if the man thought he was a wandering bum. It was better than telling him that he and his drunken brother had just sold a truckload of hooch around the countryside and were driving down the road recklessly when he flew out of the truck and was lost. At that moment, being a bum felt like a step up to Beau. Being a bum was better than a law-breaking hooch pedaling crazy man.

The breakfast was so tasty and Beau so hungry that he ate it fast, and he was done in no time. Frank had chores and animals to tend to, and Beau had to be on his way. He thanked the farmer and asked him which way was to town. Beau didn't know which town; he was so lost and turned around.

"If you go south, that way," pointed Frank, "the road goes to Floraville, then on the Marysville." Just as Beau had thought that was the way to go, if he had climbed up the embankment and got on the road back where he flew out of the truck. So that had to be the way Jess was driving then to get home.

Beau thanked the farmer and began walking down the lane, at the end of it; he turned left to walk along the county road. He carried the gun pointing down so he would not look threatening in case a car or truck did happen to pass him and offer him a lift into town, but no car came up behind him heading his way.

Beau walked for what felt like more than the five miles Frank had said it was to the town of Floraville. He kept thinking the name of the town rang a bell, but dismissed it as probably being a way that he and Jess had taken before to drive up north. It just seemed like he had heard someone mention that town before. Oh well, maybe it was one of the hooch customers who knew someone who lived there and mentioned their names. It took him a while, but he finally made it to town.

He walked through the town a ways, and decided that Floraville was somewhat larger than Marysville. He saw the name of Floraville on the water tower. Not much to the town he thought, bigger than Marysville, though. He walked down Main Street and saw three or four blocks of side streets in either direction off of Main Street. Main seemed to be more than a mile long, as far as he could figure. It looked like a nice little town. He walked nearly to the other end, and then decided to hold his thumb out when he saw a car coming up behind him. The man driving the old Model T Ford saw him and pulled over to the side of the road. The man leaned over to look out the open passenger window.

"Where you headed?" the driver asked.

"I'm headed south," said Beau, "I'm going to Marysville. I know it quite a ways down the road yet."

"Yeah, hop on in. You can ride with me. I'm headed that way myself. Could use the company," the man offered.

"The name is Jim. Jim Franklin. I'm a salesman, as you can tell," Jim had to move stuff off the front passenger seat and throw it in the tiny backseat so there was room for Beau to get in and sit down, which Beau gladly did. He was tired from walking and his body hurt all over. He got in and made sure he shut the car door well. One tumble out of a moving vehicle was enough for one lifetime Beau thought.

"Yeah, I'm a salesman," smiled Jim, "I sell brushes and brooms and cleaning products and other household items."

"Well, that sounds like a good job to have," Beau said and meant it. And then he thought how familiar that all sounded. A salesman, where had he heard something about a salesman? He must have knocked his head harder than he thought when he flew out of the truck. Yet, the mention of a salesman rang a bell somehow. Oh, now he remembered, that drunken brother of his said his wife, Joan, ran off with a broom salesman. Well, Beau sure couldn't blame her for leaving him. Jess had turned into a sorry sight for sore eyes all right, being drunk all the time. Beau sat quiet and still for a few minutes enjoying the ride and the rest; he was beat after walking for miles. It was good to sit, even though the ride was bumpy as hell. He was jerked back into reality when Jim asked if he lived in Marysville.

"Yeah I sure do, I work at the gas station, pumping gas and working on cars," said Beau. "The station that's in the center of town," he added.

"Oh yeah, I get gas there. I usually make this route about once a month," Jim said as he looked straight ahead, his eyes never leaving the road; his hands gripped the steering wheel as he talked. He was a careful driver. He had to be careful, since he was on the road all day, and every day. He made his living driving a car, and he couldn't afford to wreck it.

"You have a nice car here," Beau said thinking it was very neat and clean. He appreciated nice things and meeting nice people. He could tell the salesman took pride in his appearance, his car and his work.

"Oh yeah, got lots and lots of miles on it. The odometer done went around once already and it's on its second spin," he chuckled. Jim patted the dash with love and appreciation as one would pat a faithful dog's head.

"She's taken me many a mile," smiled Jim, "old and faithful, I call her." Jim was only too glad to have someone to talk to. Most times he drove all alone. He enjoyed the company and told Beau as much.

"Well I certainly appreciate the ride," Beau replied with a smile.

"I have a big route around several counties and spend a lot of time alone on the road," Jim said and went on, "Oh, I have regular customers so I talk to them but it's driving all alone that gets to me."

"No wife or girlfriend, to join you?" Beau asked curious now, after remembering that Jess said Joan ran off with a salesman.

"Oh, no, there's no lady, no Mrs. Franklin. Guess I'm never in one place long enough to have a wife. Not that it wouldn't be nice." Jim laughed then, "Oh, I have some girlfriends along the route. That's only natural," and not taking his eyes off the road, Jim laughed as if he was thinking about one of them at that very moment.

So, guess this wasn't the man that Jess's wife ran off

with like Jess said she did. Beau couldn't help it. He had to ask.

"You don't know anyone in Marysville named Joan, do you?" asked Beau.

"Joan. No can't say I do. Wait. I sold a broom to a lady name Joan I think. Nice lady."

"She didn't run off with you did she?" Beau just had to ask.

"What?" Jim burst out laughing. "Yeah, I'm such a good looking guy, that I have to constantly fight the ladies off me," smiled Jim, he thought Beau was kidding. Jim was short, round and bald. He was shy around the ladies, except when he was selling Watkins products, that is, then he had something to say.

"Well the reason why I ask, is that my brother says that his wife ran off with a salesman," smiled Beau. Beau never did really believe that story. Now Beau thought maybe he should have paid more attention to what his brother said when he does tell him something. It is a rare event when he did. So maybe Joan did run off with a salesman. It just wasn't this guy. It wasn't impossible. Joan had no family there in Marysville herself, so if she was unhappy why should she stick around? Jess had met Joan in another town while making deliveries for the feed store. Beau was trying to think of what the name of that town was. Oh well.

"I appreciate you giving me a ride," Beau said again. "I know I'm all dirty. Hope I am not getting your seats dirty."

"Oh, no problem. Hey, I got the cleaner to clean it,

if it is dirty, and the brush too. Can always do with a demonstration for a customer. You know the ladies like that," Jim smiled, "might come in handy for selling products. I do demonstrations all the time for the ladies in their homes. You know like clean a spot on their carpet. Then that spot is clean and makes the rest of the carpet look really filthy. It's a guaranteed sale then. They have to buy the product to clean the rest of the carpet," laughed Jim. "Something I learned in selling a long time ago. The produce is good though, so the ladies really don't mind all that much. Yep, they call me the Watkins man. I've been selling their products for years." Jim briefly removed one hand from the steering wheel to straighten his bow tie. He cocked his head with pride. He thought he looked good in his new light blue seersucker suit. He was spotless, and said that he had to be.

"Guess you have to be if you sell cleaners," Beau reasoned. He made Beau feel really filthy dirty and nasty.

"Well, here we are in Marysville. Where can I drop you off?" asked Jim.

"Oh, let me out up there at the filling station. I sure do appreciate the ride and the conversation," said Beau. He had to admit that it was good to get another person's point of view and step into their life, even if just for a moment. He felt the same way when he visited the farmer, and the farmer was kind enough to cook him breakfast.

Jim pulled the car over. Beau reached in the back

seat floor and retrieved his rifle, thanked the man again and shut the car door as he waved good-bye. Jim drove off and turned at the next block. Beau figured he was heading to a customer to make a delivery. Jim, the salesman, didn't know it then, but this visit to Marysville would not be the usual humdrum visit.

***

"What the hell happened to you?" Beau heard his boss say as he walked into the garage.

"I admit I'm a little dirty, but I'm ready to go to work." Beau had missed several days of work. He was lucky to have an understanding boss.

"Okay, good. I've been working on this old heap and I can't seem to find out why it won't keep running. I checked the spark plugs and distributor wires. Maybe you can take a look at it while I go and pump gas for that fella who just pulled up to the pump."

"Sure, be glad to," said Beau and went to work. He really wanted to check in on Mary. He figured she would be at home or in the beauty parlor working. But he thought he better do what his boss wanted. He would just have to work out the day and then go home.

***

"Where in the hell have you been?" Mary asked as soon as he poked his head in the beauty parlor door. She had been worried sick.

"Well when I got into town, Ralph put me to work right away at the filling station," Beau explained.

"What the hell happened to you? You look like you have been rolling around in the dirt," said Mary.

"I have been rolling around in the dirt," confessed Beau. He was serious, but was too tired go into details, so that was all he said about it.

"Go get cleaned up," suggested Mary, "and I'll wash those clothes." Mary turned to wash her combs and brushes and then remembered to give Beau a message.

"Jess came in here looking for you, he just wandered in, when I wasn't looking," said Mary, "You can imagine how scary that was with him standing behind me, staring and looking over my shoulder," said Mary. "He's as scary as hell."

"That son-of-a-drunken bastard. He better not keep bothering you." Beau was mad. Jess was acting strange lately. Beau thought the booze must have been getting to him.

"Well good thing Sheriff Cooper follows him around. Keeps an eye on him," said Mary, insinuating that at least she had someone who looked after her when her husband wasn't around.

"Jess sure scares me," Mary sounded scared. She was trying to get the point across to Beau to take Jess's actions more seriously. Mary felt that Beau was not taking her concerns serious enough, and would he ever? Her intuition was telling her there was a reason she should be afraid of Jess. Intuition, hell. He beat up Joan, didn't he? Mary had sworn to Joan that she would not say anything to Beau about what Jess did to her. She was afraid Beau would confront Jess. Mary had vowed to keep the secret, and she was always true to her word.

"He's been acting awfully strange," Beau had to admit.

"And where is Joan?" asked Mary. "Does Jess ever talk about her? It's like she disappeared into thin air. I never see her anymore. Marge at the dry goods store where Joan used to help out, says she hasn't seen Joan in a long time." Mary drilled Beau hoping she could learn more. But, apparently Beau knew only a little more than she did.

"Jess done said that Joan ran off with a salesman," said Beau, "and that is all I know."

"Well, I hope she did run off with a salesman and got the hell away from that crazy man." Mary was keeping the secret for Joan no matter if Beau was her husband. Women had to stick together and trust their instincts.

Beau washed up, changed into clean clothes and was bringing his dirty clothes to Ruth in the beauty parlor, when Jess burst in the door.

"You coming with me?" Jess stuck his head in the door when he saw Beau through the front window. Mary and Beau both jumped when the door burst open.

"I'm heading up to the cabin," announced Jess, not saying hello to either Beau or Mary. It was as if he was all steamed up and crazy. Mary and Beau looked at each other with raised eyebrows.

"Why you going up there?" asked Beau hoping that Jess had not heard his and Mary's conversation from outside the door. They were talking loud, and after all the walls were thin.

"I want to get another batch distilled to prepare for next week's haul." Jess said and as if he thought of something, he added, "Hey what the hell happened to you anyway? I thought you disappeared on me — into thin air."

"We can discuss that later," announced Beau then tried to change the subject, but Mary interrupted.

"What's he talking about?" asked Mary, first looking at Beau then at Jess, her eyes insisting on an answer.

"Oh. Nothing. The man's crazy, that's all," said Beau as he turned to follow Jess out the door leaving Mary alone, again.

She was lucky if she got to see him for five minutes at a time, anymore. Their situation was getting old; Mary was getting tired of her life. Lately each time she received a letter from her sister, reporting on how well things were going in Floraville for the three ladies, she envied them and wished that she could join them. It sounded like they had become close friends. Joan helped Ruth in the pastry shop and Helen had her own dry goods store. Mary was jealous. Oh she loved the beauty parlor work and it kept her busy enough. Most of the ladies were nice and easy to please. But, she could open a beauty parlor just as easily in Floraville as in Marysville, she thought. Suddenly she had an idea.

Betty, one of Mary's regular weekly customers had expressed an interest in becoming a beauty operator and running a beauty parlor like Mary's. Mary decided she would train Betty. And when Betty was trained, Betty could run the beauty parlor in Marysville and she would tell Beau that she was going to visit her sister, Ruth, in Floraville for a while.

And then while she was there, she could open a beauty parlor in Floraville. She had certainly saved enough money to do it. She quickly wrote Ruth a letter asking her to find her a location on Main Street, with a storefront. Between customers, she ran the letter to the post office and dropped it in the outgoing mail slot. She was getting excited now. Her spirits had suddenly been lifted. The ladies in Floraville had reported already that the one and only beautician there was older and about to retire. And she did not know how to do the new modern hairstyles, as Mary did. Women wanted their hair to look like the latest lady magazines, like *Vogue* and *Ladies Home Journal*.

Floraville, being a county seat, had a nice big library with magazines and a daily newspaper from Springfield. Floraville was growing and extending their city limits. The county was even building bigger and better roads leading there to draw more businesses to their community according to the town's business bureau.

Mary was eager now to work hard and save more money as she trained Betty. Betty learned quickly and couldn't wait to start working in the beauty parlor and making her own money. Mary ordered another styling dresser and chair for Betty, so they could work together. Mary could observe and train her while they both worked on customers. And after Mary was gone and Betty's business grew, she could always train another beautician to work with her using the other styling station. A well thought out plan was in place and the ladies were excited.

Chapter Twelve

Sheriff Cooper was keeping a close eye on Jess and Beau; the state district attorney was pressuring sheriffs to crack down on bootleggers. They had been too lenient he said. It seemed the governor expected the Feds and the sheriffs to track down Amendment Eighteen Prohibition violators. More deputies were hired. The captain assigned Cooper to keep an eye on Jess and Beau.

So he followed them, being careful to stay far enough back so they wouldn't suspect. He followed them that night from Mary's beauty parlor as they left in their truck and headed out of town the back way. He stayed far behind, driving his own personal truck so he would not arouse suspicion. He followed them as they drove about five miles and then suddenly turned left off the main road and drove through a grassy field. Cooper passed the field and drove on. He did not follow them. After a bit he turned his truck around, pulled over and waited on the side of the road. He got out and back tracked on foot. In the moonlight he could track their truck tires in the mud through the field. The truck tracks disappeared in the creek. The road ended and there was nothing but thick woods on the other side of the creek. What? He was puzzled until he decided to walk along the creek, and then he saw it. A road, on the other side of the creek, wound up the mountain side. He could see what looked like fresh tire tracks in the mud on the other side of the creek. Water was still sitting in the tire tracks nearest the creek.

"Well, I'll be damn!" Cooper said out loud. He barely heard his own voice in the night over the noise of the bullfrogs and tree frogs singing their nightly songs. Two owls carried on a conversation in the distance on either side of him as he walked back to his truck to sit and wait for however long it took for the two men to return. He planned to drive up the mountainside as soon as he saw Jess and Beau leave the area. He walked back to his truck hidden in the roadside weeds and covered by tree limbs. If anyone were to pass they would think he was a hunter, or the truck broke down, or he was just some guy who pulled over to sleep for a spell.

It was near dawn when he saw headlights leaving the creek and driving through the field to the main road. They turned right onto the county road opposite from where he sat in his truck. They didn't even look his way. Cooper could see that the truck sat lower, as if it was weighted down. He knew right away they were hauling hooch. Bits of straw blew out of the back of the truck as it rumbled along down the county road toward town. The engine labored as the driver shifted gears. Yep, apparently they were making a run. They were probably going to turn on the road that circled town and then head north to make their deliveries. They would be gone for a while probably, at least two days, he thought. He had plenty of time to snoop around.

Cooper slipped his truck into gear and turned right into the field. He was a little apprehensive about driving through the swift moving creek, but they just did it, so he gave it a try. The creek had a solid rock bed. Easy does it. He drove across the creek at an angle and saw the road on the other side. He hoped his wheels wouldn't start spinning on the rock or in the mud. The tires on his truck were fairly new, so he felt pretty confident driving through the creek and up the hill. When he pulled out on the other side of the creek it was easy going.

He slowly followed the road, which twisted and switch-backed up the mountainside. The road was hidden well through the trees. There was no way anyone was going to see this road from the county road below, not even in winter when the trees were bare. The road was well planned by whoever cleared the trees and brush to build it. It had to take a long time to do. As he proceeded up the mountainside, Cooper had a funny feeling it was probably their Pappy Hank who built the road, and the distillery years ago.

That is, before he robbed the bank in the next county and got himself and his wife killed, so the story goes. Cooper wasn't there. He only heard stories. He was too young at the time. But it stirred something in him, and it was one of the reasons he decided to become a deputy sheriff. There was just something about the good guys going after the bad guys that gave him an adrenaline rush.

He drove for a while, then came upon a clearing. He was amazed to see a well-kept cabin. Beau wasn't so bad, he didn't drink nor smell like booze all the time like Jess did. Saloons and breweries were all closed up because of prohibition, so they had to be either buying it or making their own hooch. Cooper suspected the latter was true, especially after he just saw the loaded truck pull out and labor down the road.

Cooper kept creeping slowly up the winding and twisting narrow road until he was near the top of the mountain, what they called the bluffs above the Mississippi River.

Cooper brought his truck to a halt in the grassy yard next to the log cabin. He got out and looked around and saw the fresh tracks from Beau and Jess's truck tires. He walked up to the cabin and onto the porch, and tried the door handle. The door was unlocked. So, he cautiously went inside, looking behind the door. As his eyes adjusted to the dim light, he saw that there were two bedrooms to the cabin and a loft area. He knew there had to be an entrance to a cellar, somewhere. Finally he found the door in the floor and lifted it up and saw the stairs leading down. He propped the floor door open against the wall. He turned on the flashlight and carefully headed down the steps. He got down in the cellar and thought he smelled a slight sour smell. But, there was nothing in the cellar. Only canned peaches in jars stacked on shelves. Damn. Here he thought that he was on to something big.

The cellar did not appear to be the full size of the cabin. What did that mean? Was there a secret room? He examined the inner wall, nothing looked like an opening. He even shined the flashlight on the outer walls, and it looked like there was another way in from the outside. So there had to be a way down to the secret cellar from up in the yard. He went back up to the main floor, stepped outside and walked around the perimeter of the cabin. Finally, behind thick bushes he saw the outside cellar doors. He tried one; it was unlocked. He pulled it up and laid it open. He was confused because it led right back down to where he was. He was puzzled.

He even looked around the yard to see if tire ruts led to another part of the yard. Maybe there was another building. He walked around peering deep into the woods. There it was—it looked like a cistern cover. He pushed the heavy metal cover off exposing steps leading to a short passageway tunneled under the yard to the secret cellar under the cabin.

"Well, I'll be damn," Sheriff Cooper said out loud. He turned his flashlight on again and headed down the steps. "Holy crap!" The light reflected on not one, but two, distilleries. He saw a gasoline generator and a pump leading outside to a well. There were small butane tanks hooked up to the boiler, an exhaust piping systems that lead up and out into the woods, down wind. It was amazing! The walls to the main cellar had to be twelve inches thick he guessed. This was certainly a well-planned setup. He never would have discovered it if he had not suspected them in the first place by their boozy smell or seen the loaded-down truck leave and had put two and two together.

Chapter Thirteen

Mary needed some thread in order to darn some of Beau's socks. So while she had time between customers, she put a note on the door, saying what time she would be back, and walked across the street to Marge's dry goods store to get some black and gray thread. When she got inside Marge was busy waiting on someone, so she looked around at the spools of thread and the material. Finally Marge was free and walked over to where Mary was looking through things.

"Can I help you find something?" Marge asked.

"Oh, I just need a couple of spools of thread. I need to darn a couple pairs of Beau's socks. He's always wearing holes in them it seems."

"Beau is Jess's brother, right? Has Beau ever mentioned anything about Jess's wife, Joan?" Marge sounded concerned. "She just up and quit on me."

"Well, not really." Mary's stomach tightened up. She didn't really want to talk about Jess or Joan.

"The other day, I passed Jess on the street. Boy, did he smell of booze. Wonder where he's getting the booze? Anyway, I asked him about Joan. And he told me some crazy story about Joan running off with a salesman that came to town. The only salesman I know is Jim Franklin, the Watkins salesman. Do you think she ran off with him? He's a short little bald headed guy who wears seersucker suits and a bow tie."

"Oh, my. I don't think I've seen him around town," replied Mary.

"Well, have any of the ladies who come into your beauty parlor said anything?" asked Marge looking at Mary inquiringly. She was distracted suddenly when she heard the bell above the store door and turned her attention to it.

"Oh my, here's Jim now. I didn't expect him until next week," announced Marge.

The little bell above the door jingled loudly as Jim opened the door while trying to manage several boxes. He closed the door with his elbow.

"Hi, Marge. I know I'm early, but your orders came early and I had other deliveries in the area, so I thought I would deliver them. How are you today?" Jim smiled at Marge and nodded at Mary. Mary wanted to pay for her two spools of thread and get back to her beauty parlor. But Marge began handling all the boxes and turning them around as if she had forgotten what she ordered. Marge and Jim began talking about this and that and the weather and not paying any attention to Mary.

She was about to put the spools of thread back on the counter when she heard Marge ask the salesman about Joan. Just like that, out of the blue, she asked him. Mary's stomach turned into knots.

"Jim I hope you don't mind if I ask you a question. But I had a woman working here with me and she disappeared off the face of the earth. Her husband, Jess, says that she ran off with a salesman that regularly comes to town. Would that be you?" Marge was smiling and almost sounded like she was kidding, but she was serious. Jim looked at her strangely.

"You know, you are the second person to ask me."

"Well, who was the other person?" Marge wanted to know.

"Oh, that would be, let me see. I believe he said his name was Beau. A fellow who lives in town here."

"Well, Beau is Jess's brother," explained Marge, "Jess is married to Joan."

"Well, why don't you ask Jess where his wife is. She surely is not with me," Jim was beginning to sound a little aggravated, "I can assure you of that."

"I have to go, Marge," Mary had put the spool back and was hurrying out the door. "I have to go, I have a customer coming," Mary said as she raced towards the door. She opened the door and ran smack into Jess, who was staggering down the sidewalk, toward her place probably, she thought. He smelled awful. Marge heard the commotion and stood in the door way. Jim was right there, too.

"Jess, where in the hell is Joan?" asked Marge, "I have a paycheck to give her."

"Well, hell, I'll take it," Jess staggered and slurred his words while reaching out his hand toward Marge, "I can always use some money." Jess then slipped and about knocked Marge over. She had to catch herself from falling to the floor.

"Hey buddy! Watch what you're doing, will you?" Jim yelled at the drunk.

"Who in the hell are you?" Jess smirked.

"He's the man who ran off with your wife," shouted Marge sarcastically. She was sorry as soon as she said it.

Jess's face grew bright red and Jim's eyes grew big and about popped out of his head. Mary turned to leave, but then Sheriff Cooper stood there blocking her way. Cooper had been following Jess.

"Just what is going on here?" demanded Cooper when he heard the yelling.

"Where is my wife, you bastard?" shouted Jess at Jim, demanding an answer. Jess was so messed up in his lies, he actually believed Joan ran off with the salesman.

"Yeah, where is Joan?" Marge yelled at the salesman.

Mary wanted to get out of there, but she was surrounded now and they were blocking her way. Before she knew it Jess took a swing at Jim and hit him square in the jaw, and Jim collapsed on the floor.

Marge screamed.

Jess was shouting, "Where is my wife?"

Mary thought Jess must have truly lost his mind, because she knew Jess put Joan in the river. Helen found her and drove her to Ruth's house in Floraville. Yet she could not say any of this. Had Joan lied? Did she indeed run off with a salesman? Did the salesman put her in the river, and Joan said it was Jess. Mary was dizzy with doubt now.

Jess was mad as hell. Marge was angry and scared, and Jim the salesman looked like he was in shock. Then Beau walked in the door. *Who else was going to show up – Joan?* wondered Mary.

"Jess, you are under arrest," announced Cooper as he swung Jess around and threw him against the counter. He pulled his arms behind him and slapped handcuffed on him.

"Hey what's going on?" asked Beau.

"You are under arrest too, Beau," smirked Cooper, "turn around and put your hands behind your back. Now!" The sheriff ordered, and Beau did what he was ordered to do.

"My god, what's going on?" yelled Mary, but no one paid any attention to her. She might as well have been invisible the way they seemed to look right through her.

"You are both under arrest for illegally selling hooch," said Cooper.

"We weren't selling hooch. What are you talking about?" Jess lied and tried to act innocent.

"You are selling hooch. You got it spilled all over you. You reek of it. I've seen you two heading out of town toward the north with the truck loaded down. And you're drunk all the time," shouted Cooper. "That is proof enough for me. I'm locking you both up."

By then another sheriff deputy had arrived with his gun drawn and led Beau and Jess outside and over to jail.

"Get the hell out of here," Cooper demanded of the salesman. And Jim ran out of the store without so much as turning back to say good-by to his customer, Marge.

"Holy cow, what a day," said Marge as she sat down in a chair, "and I still did not find out what happened to Joan."

Mary's nosy customer was walking up the street looking for her, so she left the dry goods store and led the lady back over to the beauty parlor.

"My, what's going on?" the lady asked looking concerned.

"Oh, nothing much. My husband and his brother just got arrested for bootlegging."

"Oh, my. Well? Are you still going to style my hair?" The woman asked.

"Of course. I need to stay busy," answered Mary, and then added, "Besides, the boys brought this on themselves."

Chapter Fourteen

Several days passed, and Mary was confused and upset. She never visited Beau in jail. She was mad at him. She continued to fix ladies' hair and save her money. Each day she checked the mailbox and looked for a letter from Ruth. Finally, she received one. She quickly went back inside and sat down and torn open the envelope. Ruth had written that she found a location for Mary to open her beauty parlor. Mary was so excited that things were working out. She couldn't wait to leave town. Betty, her trainee, had been doing just fine learning all the latest styles, coloring procedures, and permanent waving techniques. Mary had Betty do her own customer's hair while she watched. It was okay with the ladies if Betty did their hair instead of Mary.

Mary burned Ruth's letter and wrote a return letter to Ruth. She hurriedly put it in the mail box and put up the flag for the post man. She went back to work in the beauty parlor. She finished work late in the evening, ate supper alone and sat in her sitting room to darn Beau's socks. It was quite a pleasant evening until she thought she heard shots fired. Suddenly the back door to the house busted open and Jess rushed in. Mary was frightened out of her wits, and before she could realize what was happening, Jess was demanding she come with him. She didn't know if something had happened to Beau or if she was going to end up with Jess's hands around her neck.

"Get up! You're coming with me, honey," Jess shouted, and then grabbed Mary by the arm, pulled her up out of the chair and led her outside. She tried to fight him off, but he was too big and strong. She screamed for him to let her go as he dragged her out the back door and toward the truck. He opened the truck door and shoved her in.

"Shut up! Get in there," and he pushed her in ignoring her pleas.

"What happened? Where's Beau?" she cried too afraid to move as he gave the engine a quick crank, got in and slammed the truck into gear.

"Just keep quiet!"Jess screamed at her. He wasn't going to tell her Beau was dead; that Jess had managed to get the deputy's revolver when he opened the cell to give them food. Jess shot several shots. He hit the deputy, and a bullet hit Beau in the chest, as he got in the way between Jess and the deputy. Jess didn't mean to kill Beau, or did he, he wasn't sure. He only knew that Beau was getting on his nerves. He was going to take Beau with him. But Beau got in the way of a bullet so Beau and the deputy were dead. Deputy Cooper wasn't there at the time, he was out on rounds, or otherwise he would have gotten killed too. It would be Sheriff Cooper who would be after Jess, so Jess knew he had to get out of town fast, and he wanted to take Mary with him. Jess knew the safest place was the cabin on the mountain. No one knew about the cabin, or so he thought.

Jess drove like a maniac. He needed booze, that's what he needed, he wasn't thinking clearly. He should have headed out of town alone. But he did not want to go alone. He wanted Mary. He had always wanted Mary. Maybe, just maybe, Beau was not killed by accident. Jess wanted him out of the way so Mary would be his. Everyone always thought Beau was the better brother. Pappy Hank always said Jess should be more like Beau, even though Jess was the older brother. Beau always got what he wanted and he stole Mary from him. Well, now Beau was gone, and Mary was his.

It took a while to get out of town. It was dark and he was driving as fast as the old truck would go. They were bouncing around. Jess was taking the curves too fast. Mary screamed when Jess suddenly turned left off of the road and into a field. She screamed even louder when he drove through the creek, thinking he wanted to kill them both. Jess laughed uncontrollably as she screamed.

"Honey, you haven't seen nothing yet," Jess hollered and let out a big yell, as if he was riding a bucking bronco, as they bounced and twisted in their seats in the old truck heading up the mountainside. Mary thought that she was going to faint with fright.

Finally they got to the cabin. He stopped the truck and dragged her onto the porch and through the door. He pushed her onto the floor to get her out of the way while he looked for hooch. He couldn't find a jug, and he was going crazy. So he pulled her up and dragged her around the yard to the secret entrance to the cellar where the distilleries were. He pushed her onto the cold damp concrete where she lay crying. He laughed when he eyed a jug, pulled the cork and raised it up resting the weight of it on the crook of his arm as he took a big swig of the precious powerful medicine that gave him life.

"Damn, that's mighty fine hooch," he hollered. "Want some, little lady?" And then he stuck the jug in her face. She turned her head not wanting to even look at him. He laughed a vicious laugh, then smiled showing crooked yellow teeth and his crazy eyes lit up with an idea that popped into his hooch driven brain.

"Maybe you can help me," he crooned with an evil smirk. "I need to make more hooch for the run this weekend. Can't let my customers down. Besides, I need the money." He looked around and found a tin cup. He held Mary's jaw with one hand while he poured hooch in her mouth with the other. She choked, but he knew some got down her throat.

Then he showed her what she had to do. He showed her how to put fuel in the generator and start it up. He showed her how to get the distillery boiler going and start the electric pump for well water to flow through the system. He got the bags of ground grain mixed with water to cook into mash. He showed her step-by-step how it was done. She was going to have to help whether she liked it or not. It was a two person job. It was why he brought her out there with him. Well, and the fact, that he just like looking at her and having her around.

They worked well into the night, until he got tired. Then he led her upstairs and got out the smoked ham and bread, with hooch to wash it down. After eating, he locked her in the spare bedroom. She beat on the door for a while demanding he let her out of there. She soon realized that it was useless and settled down. He went to sleep in the other bedroom. He told himself that he left her alone out of respect for his brother; it was the least he could do, since he shot him dead and all. Pappy Hank and his mama didn't raise a totally mean bastard. He was dead tired and it didn't take him long to fall asleep. He thought of her until he dozed off.

The distillery cooked all night. He pounded on the door and woke her up before dawn. They ate ham and bread again, then went to work filling all the empty crock jugs with hooch. Of course he sampled a fair amount. He kept the revolver handy in the waistband of his pants and warned her not to try anything stupid. She knew he killed the deputy and Beau. He had to have killed them both. Or maybe the deputy killed Beau. Anyway, she knew Beau had to be dead, otherwise he would have been here helping Jess at the distillery instead of her.

Mary knew Jess always had feelings for her. Of

course, she knew, he was always telling her he did. She helped him work because she had no choice. She only hoped he wouldn't leave her locked up in the cellar when he went to sell the hooch. She was sure she would go crazy down there. The walls had to be very thick, and no one would hear her scream or even know that she was down there. So she behaved and did what she was told. She knew she had to be careful, that he was unpredictable and anything could set him off. He killed Joan, didn't he? Well, he thought he killed Joan. So she behaved as best as she could. She was not used to drinking and he kept giving her some to taste asking her to make sure it was good. More, he kept telling her to drink more. She was feeling woozy from the alcohol, but she had to keep working and doing what he said.

Chapter Fifteen

"Hey we got a letter from Mary," Ruth called to Joan. Joan was busy pulling pastries out of the oven. It was early morning and they were about to open the pastry shop. Soon the regular customers would be coming through the door.

"What did she say?" asked Joan setting the hot pan of pastries on the counter.

"She said to go ahead and get the space ready for her beauty parlor. She said Betty was doing fine and would be able to run the beauty parlor in Marysville, while she started up one here." Ruth was all excited to have her sister come, and not only visit, but to actually stay and get her shop set up. Mary had given Ruth a list of things to order and have delivered for her new beauty parlor in Floraville. Ruth was happy to help out.

"Hi, Helen," called out Joan, "Well, the whole gang's here now, and we're ready to sell pastry," Joan was as happy as happy could be. She and Ruth, were happy living together, their friendship had grown into a very special love relationship. Helen saw how happy they were and was happy for them but a little jealous. It would be nice to have someone special in her life, too.

Chapter Sixteen

"Come on, you can do it. We only have a couple more jugs to put in the truck," laughed Jess. He had hooch to drink and a fair supply to sell, so he was happy.

"Make sure you hide those jugs good in the straw," he ordered, "and make sure there is enough straw underneath the jugs. We can't have those jugs break and booze pouring out of the truck bed smelling up the county attracting the law."

Mary did not say a word and went about her business working and doing things as she was ordered. She was only too glad to be above ground and out of that horrible cramped dark cellar. It gave her the creeps being down there alone with Jess. She also had her share of hooch samplings, so she was not feeling any pain, either, and for that she was glad.

Jess stumbled over a big rock as he turned and picked up another jug. He held a jug in one hand and his own tasting jug in the other and didn't want to drop either of them. He screamed like a girl when he tripped, lost his balance and fell to the ground gracefully. He was careful not spill a drop of booze out of the jug he was sipping from, or break the one he was handing her. She wanted to burst out laughing, but she knew she couldn't. She just didn't want to let on that being a little drunk she really wasn't that afraid of him any longer. She knew she had to go along with his wishes and wait for the right moment to make her move to freedom.

Chapter Seventeen

When Deputy Cooper got back to the jail after he completed his rounds, he found the shock of his life. The jail cell door was wide open and lying on the floor were the bodies of his deputy and Beau, covered in blood. The deputy's gun was missing and so was Jess. Cooper ran out of the jailhouse and down the street toward Jess's house. As he passed Mary and Beau's house, he thought about Mary. He had to tell her that her husband was shot dead. He remembered Jess hung around Mary's beauty parlor, and suddenly, he was afraid for her, and wanted to make sure she was all right. He looked for her in the house and in her beauty parlor. She was nowhere in sight. Cooper wanted to make sure she was okay. When he couldn't find her, he decided Jess took Mary with him.

They had to be long gone by now. Beau's truck was gone, and Cooper figured that they probably headed north to hide out with one of his booze customers. He had a feeling this was going to be a long manhunt. The last few times Cooper had followed Jess to Mary's beauty parlor, he could tell that Jess wanted Mary for himself. He wondered if Jess might have shot Beau, so he could steal his wife. Cooper could tell what was going on in his head by the crazy way Jess looked at Mary, which was one of the reasons he followed Jess around town.

Cooper wondered if Jess killed Joan and buried her somewhere to get her out of the way. Sure was odd that she disappeared all of a sudden. He wasn't buying the story Jess was spreading around town that Joan had run off with a salesman. He hoped Jess had Mary with him and did not kill her, too. Jess was crazy enough to do anything, and Cooper was determined to find them, so began his search as he drove north on the main highway.

Chapter Eighteen

"Ruth, a salesman is here to see you about a delivery," called Joan.

"Won't you have some coffee and pastry while Ruth finishes up with what she is doing?" offered Joan.

"Well, sure, guess I could. It sure smells good." Jim sat himself down at a table, and he looked around. Nice place, he thought. He usually had breakfast at the Breakfast Diner, but since he had a delivery here, why not have something different this morning? The coffee was sure good.

"Damn," Jim said to himself, as he reached for a napkin in the dispenser, "spilled some on my suit. And it will really show up on this light blue color." But, he knew his fabrics and seersucker was the greatest lightweight material that cleaned up easily. He just dipped the edge of a napkin in the glass of water then padded the suite collar quickly before the coffee settled in and poof it was gone. He was so proud. He straightened his bow tie and looked at the pastry menu.

"Hi, my name is Joan, are you ready to order?"

"Yes, I am. It all looks so good. I think I'll have the cheesecake pastry."

"Oh, good choice. I made those myself early this morning. My specialty," smiled Joan, "I'll get that for you right away," and she walked away.

Joan, she said — interesting, reminds me of Marysville Joan and that crazy man who thought I stole his wife. Of all the bizarre things! Jim rubbed his sore chin still feeling crazy Jess's punch. He felt like he was being haunted. He put those thoughts aside because he had to get to work. He got out his order book, to look over the day's scheduled deliveries.

Joan came back to his table with his order of cheesecake pastry. She smiled at the look on his face when he eyed the beautiful pastry. She had to smile. She loved seeing the customers' delighted faces when she delivered their orders. Seeing them smile was worth all the hours of work she put into her craft.

"Ruth will be with you in a few minutes. She has a few things she has to take care of right way," Joan smiled an apology.

"Oh, that's fine. I'm not in a hurry," Jim replied.

"That will give you a few minutes to enjoy your pastry and coffee."

"Oh that would be perfect," smiled Jim and went on, what did you say your name was again?"

"Joan," she said with a smile, she thought she

remembered seeing this salesman in Marge's dry goods store in Marysville.

"I have the oddest story about a woman named Joan. Don't suppose you would care to hear it?" he said. He was a real talker and a people person. He hated to drive all day alone and he hated to eat alone. He thought it sure would be nice if this young lady would join him for a few minutes. "I don't suppose you would care to sit down for a bit would you. I hate eating alone."

"No not at all," Joan said as she sat down across the table from him. Actually it felt good to get off of her feet for a few minutes, and they weren't that busy at the moment. It looked like everything was under control, so she was happy to sit for a few minutes.

"Well, the last time I came through Floraville, I picked up a hitch-hiker standing along the highway on the other side of town. When I introduced myself as a salesman, he looked at me oddly. And then he asked me if I had run off with a woman name Joan from Marysville. He said her husband said his wife ran off with a salesman. He said he was this guy's brother. I tell you I had to laugh. I took the man to Marysville. And when I was in Marysville, I stopped at Marge's dry goods store, and she asked me if knew a woman named Joan, and did she ran off with me. I had to laugh at both of them. I'm not that good looking by any means. I'm short, I'm bald, I wear seersucker suits and a bow tie, for god sake. I don't think I could get a woman to just up and run off with me." Jim laughed.

But he stopped laughing when he saw Joan had the oddest look on her face.

"Oh, I'm sorry, I didn't mean to bore you," smiled Jim feeling bad.

"Oh, no," Joan said, "you don't bore me, not one bit." She looked around for Ruth. "That's an interesting story, and I would like to hear more; but, excuse me," Joan said as she got up from her chair. "I'm sorry I have to check on the pastry baking in the oven. I'll be right back. Can I bring you anything else?" asked Joan.

"No, this is delicious. I'm fine for now. Thank you, Joan," Jim replied thinking he talked too much when he got the chance.

Joan waved her hand a bit and got Ruth's attention, while she was talking to a customer, and motioned for her to follow her back into the kitchen.

"What's up? You look like you've seen a ghost, babe." Ruth looked concerned.

"I have, believe me," Joan said. "That salesman sitting over there just happened to casually tell me that Jess told his brother Beau, and other people in Marysville, that I ran off with a salesman. So they were asking this guy, since he is a salesman, if I ran off with him. He wanted to tell me the funny story since my name just happened to be Joan. Ha! Pretty funny, wouldn't you say?" Joan watched the look on Ruth's face change from content to worrisome.

"We have to get Mary out of Marysville," said Ruth sounding concerned, "and get her here with us as fast as we can." Ruth looked at Joan who was also very concerned.

Ruth hugged Joan and walked out of the kitchen. She sat down at the table with Jim to talk business. She ordered things for her pastry shop and some things for Mary's new beauty parlor. Jim was a good guy to do business with. When she sat down he didn't mention the "Joan story" to Ruth and got straight to business. Ruth thought about that story after the salesman left, and knew it was just a miracle Joan was alive and that Helen had pulled her out of the river that day. She was glad Helen was in Floraville, now she just had to get Mary there. Marysville and those Jones brothers were bad news.

Chapter Nineteen

Jess drove the truck like a crazy man, as usual. He had to fight the steering wheel that jerked in his hands with every bump and rut in the road. But the faster he got away from Marysville the better he liked it. Mary hung on for dear life. She wanted to ask him to slow down but she was afraid to, and she knew that he would not slow down just because she asked him to. She really just wanted to jump out of the truck at her first opportunity and run through the woods and fields until she found her way to Floraville. But she was totally turned around and felt lost. She only knew that they were heading north because Jess said that they were.

"Oops forgot! I guess I better slow down, so I don't break the precious cargo we are hauling," laughed Jess, as he drank booze out of a quart jar and sloshed all over himself.

It's a wonder he didn't knock his teeth out trying to drink and drive, thought Mary. She was so temped to just grab his gun and shoot him. But, he would wreck the truck since he was driving like a maniac. She knew that she had to be patient. She had another plan, which was to be friendly with him, so eventually he would let down his guard just enough so she could get away.

Jess suddenly turned off the main road down a long lane to a house. Mary wondered where they were going, but didn't say anything. She figured it out as soon as they pulled up in the yard. It was a customer's house. The man was standing in the yard, waiting. He had a beard, wore overalls and smoked a corncob pipe. He was a big man.

Mary saw a frail thin woman sitting on the porch steps. The woman must have said something when she saw the truck, because before he walked toward them, he turned around and smacked her in the face, like it was the most natural thing to do. The woman's head bounced to the side and then lowered. Mary got the feeling the slap was a display for their benefit, to demonstrate his manliness thought Mary. Whatever the reason, it made her sick to her stomach. Mary wanted to shoot him dead. God she had to get away from these people, she thought to herself, she too was a prisoner just like that poor woman. She shook now, with fear and anger.

Jess jumped out of the truck and greeted the man. He reached in the truck bed and pulled out two jugs, and handed them to him. Mary couldn't hear actually what the man said. There was a comment followed by laugher, she knew she was the butt of the joke. Then the man snorted and took a big drink out of each jug. Apparently, to make sure the hooch was of high quality. He nodded and reached into his overall's vest pocket and drew out a fist full of crumbled bills which he handed to Jess. Jess glanced briefly at the waded money, assumed it was all there and stuffed it in his pocket. He hoped it was all there; he did not want to stand in front of the man and count it like he did not trust him.

Jess thanked the man and walked to the front of the truck and gave the crank a swift turn, removing his hand just in time as the crank snapped backwards. He tried again. Contact! The Model T started up, popped and shook. Jess smiled in satisfaction and got back behind the steering wheel. He gave Mary a quick look, as he shifted the gears and they drove off to the next customer stop. Jess had his business head on today.

Mary did not say a word. She wanted to ask him about Beau, and just what had happened in the jailhouse, but was too afraid. Mary thought if Jess was really the one who killed Beau, he would not admit it, but would say that the deputy killed him. Intuitively Mary knew that Beau was indeed dead. And she knew Jess was so cold and self-centered it would not have bothered him to kill Beau. After all, he killed Joan and threw her in the river, didn't he? Mary knew that was what Jess thought happened that day. So if he was capable of killing his wife and then his brother, she could easily be next. She did not want to do anything that might set him off. She just hung on for dear life, as Jess drove like a crazy man and they bounced along the rutted road.

Mary had a lot of time to think as Jess drove in silence. She wondered why he had taken her along. She wondered what his plans were for her. Did Jess actually think that Mary was willing to be there with him? Did Jess get Beau out of the way on purpose? Mary's thoughts turned to Beau and why she was not grieving his death. Truth be told, she fell out of love with Beau not long after they were married. They only shared a house. He did his thing, and she did hers. It wasn't much of a marriage; still she was sad that his life was cut short.

Chapter Twenty

Sheriff Cooper assumed Mary was with Jess. He had no idea, which route north Jess had taken, but he was determined to find them. While he searched Mary and Beau's house looking for her, Cooper saw a photograph of Mary and Beau's wedding day. Jess was the best man in the photo. He took the picture to the newspaper office and had them make wanted posters of Jess and Mary. He took a stack of the posters with him and tacked them on posts, in church, the bank, and diners and handed them out to people on the street. His worst fear was putting Mary in danger, but he knew she was already in danger. Jess's wife, Joan, was missing, he probably killed her, but her body had not been found. Maybe she did run off like he said. That was a missing persons case he hoped would also get solved.

Sheriff Cooper drove to Lensburg and pulled up at the post office. He figured Jess was ahead of him somewhere delivering hooch to customers and then would probably keep driving. He could not come back to Marysville. He was sure if Mary was indeed with Jess, that she would realize she needed to plan an escape. Still he handed out the posters, because at this point there wasn't much else he could do.

The next town on Sheriff Cooper's list was Floraville. When he arrived, he drove down Main Street looking to the right and left and trying to decide where to stop first with the posters. Being nervous always made him hungry for something sweet. It was a wonder he wasn't a fat man, he often thought. He had a sandwich at a diner in Lensburg but it was time for a treat now. He spotted a pastry shop, which sounded good. He hoped they were open. He parked at an angle with other cars in front of the shop. He saw the "open" sign and smiled, shut off the engine and went inside. There were several customers. He walked up to the counter and laid the posters down while he looked into the glass cases filled with pastries.

"Can I help you?" Ruth asked as she smiled at the Sheriff. She saw the name Cooper sewn on his uniform. The deputy carried his patrol hat tucked under his arm as he bent over to look in the lower glass case.

"I must say, that chocolate pastry certainly looks tasty," said Cooper. He didn't know what it was called so he pointed to the one he wanted.

Ruth smiled, took a tissue in her hand and reached in for the one he wanted, as he watched intently. "Good choice," Ruth said. "You picked a good seller. A very popular item, Sheriff." She knew it was a good choice as it was one of her best sellers, and she had plenty of them freshly baked this morning. She had not seen him in the shop before. She saw he was from Marysville County.

"Welcome to Floraville. Would you like to eat it here? Coffee on the house." She smiled as she offered.

"Oh, that's a good idea, I've been driving for hours, or so it seems, and I could use a break," Cooper said as he turned to walk to a table. He was so eager to eat the delicious looking fluffy, iced, toasted brown chocolate pastry, he forgot the posters and left them lying on the counter.

Ruth noticed them and was curious. She looked down and saw the familiar face of the woman in the picture. The picture was gray and hazy yet, there was something about the woman's eyes. She was intrigued and so she picked them up to have a better look. Her heart sank when the name under the picture matched the eyes she knew all too well. Right there on the poster was a picture of her sister, printed right above her name.

"Oh, my gosh" she said out loud. She was aghast. She felt that she was going to faint. She walked over to the small table near the window where the sheriff sat. She didn't ask, just flopped in the chair next to him, holding out the picture for him to see. He looked at her oddly. She knew her face was drained of color.

"What is this all about?" asked Ruth, "that is, if you don't mind me asking."

"This man and his brother are hooch runners," said the sheriff. "This one, named Jess broke out of jail day before yesterday. Shot his brother and a sheriff's deputy dead in the process. Then on his way out of town apparently went and got this woman, his sister-in-law, from her house and took her along with him, I'm guessing."

"My god," Ruth said staring at the picture. She thought, *first Joan was a victim of Jess, now her sister Mary's was endangered by this man. And Beau was dead?*

"You look like you know these people. Do you?" asked Cooper dunking what was left of his pastry into his coffee. He stuffed it in his mouth quickly, before the coffee soaked dough fell apart. Coffee dripped and ran down his stubbled chin. He needed a shave but didn't care how he looked, he had other things on his mind like capturing Jess and Mary.

He wondered if Mary went along willingly. Of course he wondered, he was jealous. Oh, he had to admit to himself he had an interest in Mary. Evidently crazy Jess did, too. He worried for the woman. It was hard telling what Jess was capable of doing. He had killed the deputy and his own brother, who probably tried to stop him. And God only knows whatever happened to his wife who had disappeared about a year before. He looked at Ruth's face. She stared at him with painful eyes. Her eyes looked familiar now. He looked at the eyes in the picture and back at the eyes of the woman sitting across from him. Ruth knew that the sheriff saw the resemblance.

"Yes, I do know this woman. She is my sister." Ruth spoke just above a whisper as if the words were too

128

painful to spew out into the dead air that suddenly filled the room.

"What about the man?" Cooper asked his eyes lighting up with hope. "Do you know him?"

"Only that he is Mary's husband's brother" frowned Ruth. "It has been years since I visited Marysville, probably their wedding was the last time. We live busy lives. Both of us trying to keep our businesses going to make ends meet."

"They're on the run," said Cooper. "I need to find them."

"Together? I don't understand," Ruth said with tears in her eyes.

"I believe he kidnapped Mary to use as a hostage." Cooper was pretty much convinced of this. He doubted very much that Mary went with Jess willingly. Or that it was a love triangle as gossip in Marysville had it. Marge, at the dry goods store, was quick to tell Cooper she decided Jess got rid of Joan and Beau so he could take Mary; she doubted Mary went willingly. Cooper had to agree because every time he stopped by Mary's beauty parlor while following Jess around town, it appeared that Mary was very uncomfortable, maybe even afraid of Jess and the idea that he just showed up and popped in whenever he wanted.

Chapter Twenty-One

It was their third stop after what seemed endless miles of rutted bumpy roads in that beat up truck. Mary's hand felt the barrel of a rifle as she grasped onto anything she thought was stable to keep her from bouncing and rocking back and forth. She hoped the rifle was loaded, but there was no way that she could tell with it wedged down between the seat and door frame. Jess was armed with the dead deputy's revolver, which he kept in the waistband of his pants, away from her and out of her reach. He looked at her now and then, stealing a glance between fighting the rutted narrow road and trying to dodge the low over-hanging tree branches.

Again they pulled into a customer's yard. Frank and his two sons sat on the porch chewing tobacco and spitting on the ground. They walked up to the truck with their hands hanging on the bib overalls suspenders. They looked curiously at Mary, as if they hadn't seen a woman in years, or at least a city-like woman. Mary saw a ragged woman sitting in a rocker on the cabin porch. It looked like she was peeling potatoes. Three youngsters romped around her; boys, it looked like, all scruffy and dirty. Mary looked straight ahead, scared out of her wits. She kept her right hand on the hidden rifle barrel. Jess got out and reached over the side of the truck bed and dug two jugs of hooch out of the straw. The three men immediately smiled.

"Hey, how about another one for my other son? There are three of us here," the tall thin man asked with a toothless grin. He rocked with anticipation, eager to get his hands on the jugs. Jess obliged him although it may cut him short for the last stop; he wanted no trouble from the three of them.

"Give you two bits for the lady," one of the sons growled, his creepy eyes staring at Mary. Mary froze in her seat. She tightened her grip on the rifle.

"The lady's taken," Jess responded in a threatening tone, standing now on the driver side of the truck, his left hand on the gun in the waistband of his pants. The old man saw the gun then reached in his pocket grabbed some bills and pitch them in the window at Mary. He wanted the woman, but he also did not want to ruin the hooch delivery arrangement he had with Jess.

"See you next couple of weeks," Jess said quickly as each sampled their own jugs. He had left the truck running and was glad that he did. He remembered past experiences with these nasty guys and did not want to hang around any longer than he had to. The truck shook and rumbled in place, and spewed fumes and black smoke out the back. As soon as the money came flying in the window, and it looked like there was enough, Jess grabbed the floor shifter, shifted into gear and they headed down the lane as fast as the truck would go.

Neither said a word, just looked straight ahead and watched the road. Mary eased her grip on the rifle just a bit, no longer feeling threatened by the three burley, nasty men. She did not know how much more of these hooch delivery encounters she could take. She had to come up with a plan. If only she knew the area better. She had no idea where they were going and Jess was not sharing any information. She knew there were more jugs still in the back, so there were going to be several more stops.

Chapter Twenty-Two

Sheriff Cooper left a poster or two with Ruth but did not leave any in any of the businesses in the town of Floraville. He did not want to set the stage if Jess and Mary did come to town, they would be aware he was looking in that area for them. Instead, he drove out of Floraville and headed further north, thinking Jess was probably making deliveries of hooch. He doubted if Jess would stick around long in any one place. Cooper had wired the chief sheriff deputy that Beau was dead, and Jess was on the run with Beau's widow. Cooper let him know that he had deputies on the lookout for them.

Ruth went about her day cleaning up the shop, getting ready to do more baking. During the slower times of the day she baked more pastries. She had big plans for her shop and was in the process of buying the adjacent building, remodeling it and adding lunch and supper to her menus. The plan was Joan would run the pastry shop, while Ruth ran the limited lunch and supper menus in the new restaurant that would be next door to the pastry shop. Of course, more help would eventually be hired when the business grew. Floraville was growing and they were expanding to be ready for more customers.

"Joan, when you get a minute. I need to talk with you," said Ruth as she passed Joan who was stirring up batter in the kitchen.

"I have a minute now, what's up?" asked Joan as she walked over to join Ruth at a table.

"What's going on?" Joan sounded worried as she sat down next to Joan.

"Sheriff Cooper from Marysville was just here with posters of two people—a man and a woman. The man was your idiot husband, Jess, and the woman was my sister, Mary."

"What? What is going on? Why would they be together? And why was he looking for them?" Joan asked all three questions at one time and then sat quietly ready to hear all that Ruth had to say.

"Well, Jess and Beau are hooch runners, distilling and running hooch up north. Cooper arrested Beau and Jess and had them in jail. While Cooper was out on patrol, Jess grabbed the attending deputy's gun and shot both the deputy and Beau dead. He then went to Mary's house and kidnapped her, and that's about it," said Ruth.

"Well, that's certainly enough," frowned Joan. "Wonder which way they are headed. I wish he didn't have your sister with him." Joan sounded worried.

"Hearing that worried me, too. Hard telling what the fool might do. The last letter I received from Mary was the one where she said to go ahead and start getting the things here ready for her beauty parlor. Betty was all trained and more than capable to run the beauty parlor in Marysville herself."

"Jim Franklin, the Watkins salesman, has been getting in touch with his contractor friends and they are in the process of building styling stations complete with sinks and running water, electrical outlets and everything else she may need," said Ruth." We are going to stay on schedule with this. We can be ready for Jess and Mary if they happen to show up in town. If they don't come this way, we'll have to count on the sheriff to find them.

"Did you tell the sheriff about Jess trying to kill me?" asked Joan.

"No, I did not," confessed Ruth. "I was pretty shocked and worried about Mary at the time."

"That is just as well, because total surprise could really work in our favor," Joan said. The more she spoke of Jess the angrier she became, "I'd like to teach him a lesson myself, I think."

"Well, he is all yours to do as you wish as long, as we can keep Mary safe while you do it."

"I'm going to have to think about this for a while," said Joan.

"In the meantime, let's go on with our plans to expand the pastry shop into the adjacent building to offer lunch and supper," said Ruth. "And let's get Mary's beauty parlor all set up for her for when she gets here." Ruth knew in her heart Mary would be with them soon.

"Great idea, Ruth," smiled Joan. "After all, I owe Mary big time. She gave me your address and I had Helen bring me here to you. My whole world took a wonderful turn for the better," Joan hugged and kissed Ruth.

"Come on, let's update Helen." Ruth put a "back in ten minutes" sign on the door and they walked a few doors to the Helen's dry goods store, which was next door to where the builder was working on Mary's beauty parlor. Jim had found a man who fixed up a beauty parlor in Lensburg, so he was quite familiar with what needed to be done.

"Why that son-of-a-bitch!" Helen said upon hearing what Ruth and Joan told her about what Jess had done.

"Yes, I guess he's got killing in his blood after he thought he killed me," Joan smirked sounding angry.

"Ladies, I think we need to be ready for this fool, just in case the sheriff does not get him first, if he comes to town with Mary," said Joan. Helen and Ruth nodded in agreement and were ready to discuss some ideas.

"Hopefully, Mary will not mention us," said Joan, "If she does it will spoil the element of surprise."

"Yeah, but she doesn't know that Sheriff Cooper was here. Let's walk all over town and make sure none of those posters are in sight, anywhere. We don't want people recognizing them," Ruth said. "Sheriff Cooper said he wasn't going to leave any of them up out of respect for me. But I'm sure he talked to the sheriff here.

I think the idea was, if they do come to town, he wanted Jess to feel safe here, so he could surprise him."

"I hope we get our hands on him first," said Joan. Helen and Ruth couldn't blame her for feeling the way she did after Jess nearly killed her.

"Helen, you are my angel. I would not be here if it were not for you seeing me in the river and risking your life to pull me out." Joan had tears in her eyes and took Helen's hand.

"Well, I certainly will never forget that day," whispered Helen. "Come on, let's get the bastard."

Chapter Twenty-Three

The ladies made sure that all Jess and Mary posters were taken down. The local sheriff was just outside of town, at his cabin on the lake, fishing. He was pretty much out of the way all the time, and they did not have to worry about him.

There was only one hotel in town. Ruth knew the owner, Mildred, pretty well from quarterly meetings to discuss improving Main Street businesses with the other Floraville business ladies. Mildred had her own bad experiences with her drunken husband until the lord blessed her with his demise. In a drunken stupor he picked a fight with the wrong guy in the saloon. They moved the fight out to the street and Mildred's husband took a bullet right between the eyes. The town remembered it well, that was the last drunken street fight before Prohibition became law in 1920. Mildred was doing fine without him and was happy to run her hotel with her son, Josh, and a handful of employees.

"Hi Mildred, do you have a minute?" asked Ruth when she saw her working behind the hotel counter.

"Sure Ruth, what's on your mind?" asked Mildred as she followed Ruth to their usual private table in a corner away from customers.

"I have a favor to ask," Ruth said as she pulled the wanted poster out of her handbag and held it so only Mildred could see it.

"Sure, anything, I'd be happy to help." Mildred was only too happy to help Ruth—the ladies in town stuck together. "What do you have there?"

"This is my sister and her brother-in-law," whispered Ruth and continued to speak very quietly so as no one else could hear, not that anyone else was paying any attention.

"My sister's name is Mary. I've spoken of her before, she's from Marysville," said Ruth.

"Oh yes, I remember. My, what's happened?" asked Mildred.

"Jess, this guy in the poster, her brother-in-law, killed Mary's husband and has kidnapped her. Mary mentioned Jess in her letters, saying that he was always hanging around her beauty parlor, even more so after his wife Joan mysteriously disappeared." Ruth told Mildred.

Mildred was well aware that Joan's husband, Jess, tried to kill her and threw her in the river, and how Helen had found her. There was a secret bond between tragic stricken women of Floraville who knew they had to fend for themselves.

"What do you have in mind, Ruth?" asked Mildred. She knew Ruth well enough after the incident with Joan, to know that Ruth had some ideas up her sleeve that involved revenge.

"Well, I was thinking," said Ruth and went on with that determined look in her eye that Mildred had seen before. "They are on the run. They can't go back to Marysville. I believe they are driving around delivery hooch out of the back of a truck. They may keep going north, but in case they happen to come here to Floraville, I want to be ready for them. They may come here to eat and sleep. If they do come here, I want you to be ready for them," said Ruth.

"Just what did you have in mind?" asked Mildred.

"I want you to give them special rooms. Say, the only room you have available is the room with an adjourning room on the first floor, near the back door," said Ruth adding, "hopefully, Mary can figure a way to escape from him."

"Okay, I have enough rooms, I can just keep that one available and reserved only for them."

"Great!" Ruth said. "As far as other ideas, I'm afraid I do not have any right now. I have spoken to Joan, and I believe she has a few ideas of her own."

"Like what, pray tell?" asked Mildred cocking her head and raising an eyebrow signaling a combination of intrigue and conspiracy.

"Like scaring the crap out of him," Ruth said. "Joan said the man always was a little jumpy and skittish, and Joan would like to see just how skittish he really is."

"Well, how are you going to scare him without scaring Mary?" Mildred asked anxious to hear the answer.

"Well, I think we're still working out the details regarding that. If only we could clue Mary in so she could catch on right away." Ruth got tears in her eyes.

"I'll keep an eye out for these two," Mildred said looking at the picture on the poster and then patting Ruth's hand, "not to worry."

***

The days dragged by and Ruth wanted to hear something about her sister, but was afraid to ask anyone, certainly not the local sheriff; not that he would have a clue anyway. The sheriff wasn't around much of the time. If anyone needed him, they knew to find him at his cabin on the lake, fishing. Although he was more of a fisherman than a sheriff, he did supply Mildred with fresh fish for her hotel dining room.

Josh, Mildred's son, wasn't very fond of the sheriff and told his mother that he always thought the sheriff was sweet on her. Mildred just smiled at Josh, and told him he had nothing to worry about. Josh had been very protective of his mother since his dad was killed in the street shoot out. He helped her with the upkeep of the hotel and restaurant.

The business ladies kept Main Street up-to-date which helped Floraville grow. Helen's dry goods store was flourishing. She sold material, thread and everything needed for sewing, even sewing machines, which included sewing lessons. Women came from all over to buy and to learn. Next door to Helen's dry goods store was the building for Mary's beauty parlor. There was no longer a beautician in Floraville, since the one they had for years retired. Ruth had the idea to add a barbershop next to Mary's beauty parlor. She figured men would not mind a woman cutting their hair if they didn't sit next to a woman getting her hair curled. So a separate room was a good idea and Mary could always train someone to cut men's hair, Ruth thought. And Ruth's restaurant addition to the pastry shop was coming along nicely. Ruth had to hire more people to help cook and wait on tables. It was a good feeling to see prosperity come to Floraville, and the ladies were willing to do their fair share to contribute to its success.

Chapter Twenty-Four

"Son-of-a-bitch," yelled Jess, "the god-dang brakes aren't working."

The truck was tumbling down the hillside road. Jess was afraid it was about to tip over and roll all the way down. Mary held her breath and couldn't scream even if she wanted to. She was hanging on for dear life.

"Do something!" she yelled at Jess as they bounced and were thrown around.

"Like what?" Jess hollered back at her. He was doing as best as he could to keep control of the steering wheel, which jerked back and forth, nearly breaking his fingers. His wrists hurt. He pulled the brake lever—it had no effect. A rod beneath the truck had come apart driving through deep ruts in the road. Finally Jess saw an opportunity—there was an open area with tall grass, no trees and no fence. He made the quick decision to suddenly steer the truck into the grass. The truck hopped across the ruts in the road into the tall grass, which gathered under the truck and slowed it down to a stop.

Mary thought Jess's idea was brilliant, but she wasn't going to say anything. Instead, she let out a big sigh of relief. "Praise the lord," was all she could think to say.

"Whoa," Jess was ecstatic with happiness and relief. He looked at Mary and she at him and nothing more needed to be said. They had both been scared half to death. Jess jumped out of the truck. He was afraid the hot motor would catch the grass underneath on fire. It smelled hot. They had only a small jug for water and several jugs of booze left. But the booze had such high alcohol content and was one hundred proof; it only would have contributed to a fire.

"Jump and run," Jess ordered Mary.

She smelled a burning smell and saw smoke. She jumped, grabbed the rifle and took it with her. She ran off in the opposite direct of Jess. She was slim, quick and quiet maneuvering through trees and underbrush. She slipped down and crossed ditches, moving as fast as she could. She didn't hear Jess behind her, but she kept right on running. She came upon a rocky creek bed and ran through it. She heard a shot then, and something rushed through the tree leaves and buzzed past her ear. Damn he was right behind her. She didn't want to take the chance to turn around to fire the rifle at him fearing that maybe it wasn't loaded, or if it was loaded, she feared she would just waste a shot and miss him. That would only slow her down, and at the same time, give him a chance to fire at her again and catch up to her.

It was late afternoon, darkness would soon be on her side, if only she could stay ahead of him. She tried to be very quiet and slip through the underbrush, sometimes on her hands and knees. She took the opportunity to look back when she slipped and fell in a muddy area. She turned but didn't see him. He could have been hiding somewhere. She couldn't take the chance to stop. She ran through pastures and past a farm. But what she had seen of the local folks while delivering jugs of hooch made her not want to run into any of them.

She stayed on the move and avoided open roads. She heard another shot. He had to be close; revolvers don't go as far as a rifle—that much she knew. How did he ever get a clear shot unless he was close? Was she leaving tracks? She had to hide better. She was in the woods and saw deer. Maybe the shots she heard was someone hunting. She saw a tree she thought she could climb, and felt lucky to have dungarees on when Jess kidnapped her. She didn't know how, but she managed to climb the tree with the rifle.. She climbed up as high as she could until the thick limbs grew thin. She thought she would just sit up in the tree like a deer hunter and if Jess passed below her she could shoot at him.

She waited and waited until it grew dark. She dozed off and slept through the night.

***

"Ouch, son-of-a-bitch," Jess hollered. He was running with the gun and stumbled into a thorn bush and the gun went off. He backed up and fell to the ground away from the prickly bush. He checked and he had not shot himself, but he had wasted another bullet. Damn. And she got away. It was getting dark and he had to do something. He trekked through a pasture, saw the cows, then saw the barn. He decided to sleep in the barn for the night. Hopefully, the farmer would be home and fix him supper. Maybe Mary was already there in that house eating. Damn bitch. He was angry with her now. How dare she run away from him like that!

The moon was coming up on the eastern horizon, when he reached the steps to the farmhouse porch. He saw a light inside. He stuck the revolver in his belt behind him and pulled out his shirt tail to hide it, then knocked on the door. The door was yanked open and a big round man stood in the doorway holding a rifle. His overalls were ragged and his beard long. Jess saw that it was the man with the two sons who he had delivered three jugs to, two or three days before, it wasn't clear in his head which day that was. He was sorry to see the thin bent woman, his wife he guessed, in the background. Jess did not see or hear the two sons. Suddenly he was afraid and knew that he should not have knocked.

"Hello," said Jess, his voice slightly shaky.

"What do you want?" asked the tall man, lifting the rifle higher so it pointed at Jess's head.

"Just wanted to know if I could sleep in your barn tonight?" asked Jess, he knew he sounded pitiful.

"Oh, it's you. The hooch man," said the big guy as he looked out around Jess looking for the lady he had with him earlier. "Where's your little lady friend?"

"Oh, I dropped her off at her father's house," Jess lied.

"Oh, too bad," laughed the big round man.

"Where's your truck, with the jugs of booze?" he wanted to know, stepping out on the porch to look around.

"The brakes failed, I wrecked it."

"Well, you're having yourself quit a day, aren't you?" chuckled the big guy.

"Come in." He stepped out of the way so Jess could come in the house.

"Ma, fix this man a sandwich, or two." The big man barked orders at the little woman. And she quickly obeyed and began making sandwiches for Jess. Jess was feeling very uneasy. Something didn't feel right.

"I suspect you made lots of money delivering that whole load of hooch to all your customers. I seen how many jugs you had in back of that truck," the big round man growled looking down at Jess in a threatening way.

"What you talking about? I gave it to the girl to hold. I don't have any money," Jess only hoped the man believed him. He felt for the gun in the back of his belt, the handle turned towards his right hand. The man was to his left a bit; he had propped the rifle against the wall. He did not see a gun on the man or anywhere near him as he stood in the kitchen by the stove.

The woman put the sandwiches in a paper sack on

the table. He wished he could grab the bag and run. And was just about to do that, when the big man moved to stand near the door blocking his escape route. Jess just about froze. Damn. He thought, the hell with it I'm killing him. With one swift motion, he grabbed the sandwich bag with his left hand, as he pulled out the gun from the back of his pants with his right and began firing. The big man fell dead. The little woman just stood there, staring. Jess thought he saw a bit of a smile form on her thin lips as she stared at the monster of a man, lying sprawled out on the floor, dead.

Jess jumped over the dead man and ran toward the barn where he saw a truck, and quickly started it up. The hell with looking for Mary, he was getting out of there before the law came after him for killing the man. He thought he was dumb to leave a witness who could easily identify him as the hooch runner who shot her old man. He was in deep trouble and knew it as he drove down the road. Oh hell, he was in deep trouble already for killing the deputy, and Beau and breaking out of jail; not to mention distilling and selling illegal hooch.

He was lost and had no idea which direction he was going. He looked for the moon but the sky was clouded over, so he had no sense of direction. It didn't matter, the only thing he knew what to keep driving. He had the two sandwiches so there was no need to stop. He was hoping he was driving north, but he wasn't sure.

Chapter Twenty-Five

Mary slept soundly to the rhythm of the croaking tree frogs that seemed to be everywhere. She slept until the first light of dawn. She picked out the highest point in the south, in a distance as far as she could see, to help guide her. Then she climbed down from the tree and headed south. She stayed away from the road but kept it in sight to help to guide her. She knew sooner or later she would end up in a town if she followed the road. It was easy enough to walk along pastures through trees and bushes near the road.

At one point she picked some black berries and was careful of the stickers. She picked as many as she could reach and ate them all. The juicy plump berries helped both with her hunger and her thirst. She continued on. She felt brave with the rifle and walked with determination. She came upon a garden situated behind a barn far away from the farmhouse. She had walked all day and it was near dark. She had walked for miles, and her feet hurt. She sat at the edge of the garden and tore off leaves of lettuce, and pulled up carrots out of the ground. There were straw potatoes she dug up and green beans, and melons to eat. She ate her fill, and then filled her pockets with carrots and a potato or two. She slipped away from the farm and found another tree to climb and fell asleep listening to the rhythm of tree frogs down at a nearby creek.

She cradled the rifle in her arms feeling brave and adventurous, and so different from that sad depressed woman who sat in the rocker on her sunny back porch thinking her future was filled with gloom. She was strong now, she had met danger, and a strong woman rose up. No longer was she that sad ill-fated woman.

A rooster in the near distance announced the dawning of a new day, and she awoke to twinkling sunshine through leafy tree branches. She spotted the high point in the south she had picked out to guide her the day before, and she began her journey. Feeling fresh and ready to walk, she climbed down and continued to trek south. She walked and snacked on the carrots and potatoes she had in her pockets.

She walked for hours; the sun had passed the high point on the sky. Mary realized the road was becoming busier and she had to get down on the ground behind bushes or fences to hide more often. A car passed, then a truck, then another car. She knew that she was on the main road and getting closer to a town. She had no idea which town. She kept walking through tall grass, near fields and pastures. Keeping her eyes on the landscape's highest point and following the road had paid off. In the distance, she saw a church steeple. And tried to read the name of the town that was painted on the water tower, but it was still too far away. She continued to stumble through high grass on the side of a ditch away from the roadway.

Finally, she was close enough to read the name of the town painted on the water tower: Floraville. Oh my god, she was there. How did she get there? A sense of pride and achievement welled up inside of her. Suddenly she felt as if she was home, knowing her sister, Ruth, Joan and Helen would be so excited to see her. Her heart suddenly jumped with joy. She wanted to run on the road the rest of the way; but knew she still had to stay hidden until she got closer to Ruth's house. She remembered Ruth's address from the letters they had sent to each other.

She thought Ruth must have sent her more letters regarding the beauty parlor she was going to set up for her. She knew Ruth must have been wondering why she had not heard anything more from her. She couldn't wait to get there, no longer did her feet and legs ache from trekking through tall grass on uneven ground. She walked strong, with determination and joy.

By the time Ruth reached the edge of town it was dark. She was careful when she walked down Main Street so no one would see her. It was late and the street was mostly deserted with only a couple of places open. She passed the hotel. Was it her imagination or did she see Jess get out of a truck and walk into the hotel? She dreaded the sight of him. Somehow, somewhere he got himself another truck, but the man she saw was Jess all right, all roughed up and dirty. She could see through the big glass hotel window that he walked up to the counter and a woman greeted him. Mary went on her way to find her sister's house.

Chapter Twenty-Six

" Can I help you?" asked the woman behind the counter.

"I need a room for a couple of nights," Jess said to the clerk behind the counter as he reached in his torn pants pocket and pulled out a wad of bills. He thought the woman seemed pleasant enough and the place looked clean. He was planning to stay two nights; he had not slept in a bed in a long time. He was exhausted and tired from bouncing around in the truck for mile after mile. He could have sworn he was driving around in circles there for a while. He got so lost. He just got lucky to find a town. He was so tired and needed to sleep.

"I have a room available on the first floor, A1, right around the counter, that way," said Mildred as she pointed him in the right direction. Oh, she recognized his ugly face all right. She had memorized that face on the sheriff's poster. She would have recognized Jess anywhere.

"Here's the key, and my name is Mildred," she spoke kindly to him. "If you need anything, just come to the front desk and ring this bell on the counter." She smiled at him.

"Thank you," Jess quickly found the room, poured water from the bucket into the water bowl and washed up with, then fell onto the bed. He was asleep as soon as his head hit the pillow.

Mildred was already heading down the street to Ruth's house. Where was Mary though? She wondered where Mary was, because Jess was alone. What had this monster done with Mary?

***

"Ruth, it's me, let me in," Mildred said as she taped eagerly on the door. Joan got to the door first and opened it, and Mildred rushed in.

"He's here," Ruth announced in a whisper as she entered the house. "He's here at the hotel. I put him in A1 like Ruth wanted me to," said Mildred as Ruth rushed in from the other room to join Mildred and Joan in the kitchen.

"Was Mary with him?" Ruth was frantic and eager to know.

"No, I'm sorry, he was all alone," said Mildred visibly shaken.

"Oh my god, what has he done to her?" Joan asked. They all looked at each other with fear. They stood there huddled close to each other for comfort.

154

Suddenly, Mildred saw a face looking in the kitchen window. She let out a scream.

"Oh, who's that?" whispered Mildred thinking that awful man followed her there. Ruth and Joan turned to see what she was looking at and then realized that was not the face of a man. That was a woman looking in the window. Mary rushed to the kitchen door just as Ruth yanked it open.

"Come in, come in," Ruth cried. Mary ran into his sister's arms and sobbed. They stood there and held each other for the longest time, both crying.

"I thought you were dead," cried Ruth taking Mary's face into her hands and looking deep into her eyes to make sure she was all right.

"You're safe now," Joan hugged Mary. Joan introduced Mary to Mildred, the owner and operator of the hotel Jess had just checked into.

"Yes, I saw Jess pull up to the hotel," reported Mary. They all were crying now as they sat down at the kitchen table.

Ruth put a kettle of water on for tea and made sandwiches and soup while Mary took a hot bath and put on the clean clothes Ruth laid out for her. Joan ran down to get Helen so she could meet Mary. And it was time to plan their next step on how they were going to handle Jess.

***

The four ladies sat in the kitchen talking and updating

Mary on what had been going on in Floraville. They were so happy to have Mary there with them now, safe and sound. Mary asked Ruth if she got her last letter telling her to go on with the beauty parlor plans, and Ruth confirmed and said Mary would be very pleased with the beauty parlor's progress. She would show her first thing in the morning. They had so many things to catch up on. Ruth shared how she and Joan expanded the pastry shop into a full restaurant. Helen told Mary about her dry goods store and was happy to have the adjacent location reserved for Mary. Then they got down to the business of Jess and what to do about him.

"We could tell the sheriff," Mildred said, "and let him take care of Jess."

"You mean our sheriff who is never in his office but rather out at the lake fishing all the time?"

"There is no proof Jess did me any harm, or that he even tried to kill me. It would be my word against his," complained Joan.

"He killed my husband and he kidnapped me," cried Mary, "but can either of those things be confirmed? They might say that I went along with Jess willingly."

"Jess always had a thing for you Mary," Joan said, "I don't think he ever got over it."

"Well, seems to me," said Mary, "that Sheriff Cooper's word would be the only thing substantial to get Jess locked up for good. Someone killed Beau and the deputy sheriff, when Jess escaped the jail in Marysville. And Jess has the deputy's revolver. I saw it on him. He shot it at me when I was running through the woods to get away from him."

"Personally," said Joan, "I would like to scare the crap out of Jess. You know, teach him a lesson. Because I doubt he will ever end up in jail and pay for any of his crimes."

"Well, what can we do?" asked Ruth looking at the other ladies sitting around the table.

"Jess was always very superstitious. Once he thought he saw his dead grandmother at her grave site. Maybe he did. I don't know," said Joan, "but it scared the hell out of him and he wouldn't leave the house at night for the longest time after that happened to him. Maybe we can scare him to death," suggested Joan.

"Yeah, I remember one Halloween night and the headless horseman stunt that his buddies and Beau pulled on him," said Mary. "He was walking to the neighbor's at night and Beau rode by on a horse with his coat pulled up and buttoned up over his head, like his head was gone, and they poured rabbit blood everywhere. Jess wet his pants, he was so scared and he screamed all the way home. Beau laughed about that stunt for years afterwards."

"Yeah those guys were pretty cruel," said Joan, "but that gives me an idea."

"He thinks he killed you, Joan," Helen piped up.

"Yes, he does, doesn't he," smiled Joan. She thought for a moment and then suggested, "I think I'll creep into his room at the hotel and appear to him, as a ghost." Joan was kidding, but the other ladies took her seriously.

"Oh, my god! That would be perfect," Helen agreed with the rest of the ladies.

"When?" asked Mildred " I want to make sure that I'm at the front desk when he comes running and screaming out of his room." She smiled and looked around at the ladies.

"It may take me a bit to get the right ghost costume," said Joan very eager now to put a plan to the ghostly plot.

"I think I can help you with that. Let's go to my dry goods store, now," insisted Helen. "Who knows, he may decide to leave tomorrow. And it's just about midnight, the bewitching hour, it's a perfect time to sneak in and scare him."

***

The ladies went next door to Helen's dry good store to look over her bolts of material. The sheerer the better, Helen thought. She found the perfect white sheer material and cut a very large piece to drape over Joan. It covered her head, shoulder, and arms, and hung down to touch the floor. All four women agreed it was perfect.

They sneaked across the street to the back entrance of the hotel. Mildred went to the front desk and got the key to room A1 where Jess was sleeping. It was one o'clock in the morning. Joan draped the material over herself, with Mary and Ruth's help. She held a candle in her hand, so Jess could see her really good, and she would make ghostly sounds after he woke up. They were nervous, but it was now or never, they thought. They couldn't just let him just get away without any action against his evil deeds. They knew they had to be careful, and Mary reminded them that Jess had a gun.

"I want to scare him, like he scared me," confessed Joan. The ladies all agreed that she certainly had the right to her revenge since Jess, in his mind, killed her, and was just fine with that.

"Just don't get yourself killed doing it, because then you would have played right into his hands. Remember, he wanted you dead," warned Ruth.

"You're right," sighed Joan, "I'll just have to be extra careful."

They went around the darkened corner into the hall. No one was around. The hotel was half full and it appeared everyone was fast asleep. The ladies slipped the slightly transparent material over Joan's head and made sure it covered the white gown that she wore. She was barefoot so she wouldn't make any noise and to appear more spiritual. The key was quietly inserted into the lock of the door of A1, the hall was dark, so Joan could slip in the room without notice. She heard deep sleep snoring as soon as she opened the door and slipped in. The glow from the full moon was enough light for him to easily see her when he woke up.

Chapter Twenty-Seven

Sheriff Cooper drove all over the county tacking up posters in post offices and sheriff offices and any other place he could find a space. Cooper drove his squad car from town to town through the countryside. After several days he came upon an abandoned truck on the side of the road. It looks very familiar to him with straw in the bed of the truck. So Cooper reached in and around the straw and felt something hard, like stone, moved the straw away and pulled out a jug. He rested it on the back fender of the truck and pulled out the cork. Right away he smelled a distinct familiar strong fragrance—yep it was hooch, all right.

Cooper wondered if Mary was with Jess when he drove to this spot. He walked around the truck looking for clues. It looked like the truck may have run off the road out of control and that the tall grass gathered underneath and slowed it down. It appeared that the grass got hot, some of it was brown, but nothing caught fire. Cooper didn't know much about auto mechanics but if he had to guess, he wondered if maybe the brakes had failed. He looked for anything, any hint, which he could find, that would tell him if both Jess and Mary had been there.

He saw some broken branches, and flattened grass and followed the trail it made. Finally, he saw what looked to be footprints pressed in the soft earth beneath the flattened prairie grass. Some of the larger footprints looked like man size shoe prints. And he found smaller size footprints like that of a woman's size boot with a narrow heel. He walked a bit further until he saw the sun reflected on something shinny. Cooper bent over to take a closer look and upon further examination, he saw that it was an empty bullet casing that was the same caliber as his deputy sheriff's revolver.

The dead Marysville deputy's revolver was not found anywhere in the sheriff's office or jail. So Cooper could only assume that Jess took the gun with him. Did Mary try to run away and Jess fired at her? Cooper hoped if that was the case that he missed and Mary got away without getting hurt. Cooper liked Mary and would have hated to see Mary take up with Jess. The deputy could have killed Beau, or maybe Jess took the gun from the deputy then killed Beau and the deputy.

In either case Jess and Mary were missing. Cooper thought that she was probably taken as hostage, a pawn perhaps for Jess to use as a bargaining tool. Cooper was thinking of all different possible scenarios as he stepped carefully through the countryside. The trail was leading him closer to the woods and he came upon a thick tree trunk with a bullet hole, scoffed marks and snapped branches. The trail came to an end there. Cooper looked around and in the distance saw a farm. He walked back to his cruiser and followed the county road until he came upon the lane that led to the farm and drove toward it.

At the farm, Cooper got out of his cruiser and walked to the porch. As he stepped up to the porch he looked around to see if there was anyone at home. When he looked to the side of the house he saw a wooden cross marking a gravesite. The dirt looked freshly dug. The screen door opened a bit and there stood a small frail looking woman who was holding a rifle.

"You're a little late, Sheriff," said the woman. She was skinny, and gray hair outlined her wrinkled face. There was dirt and blood stains on her dress.

"What happened here?" asked Cooper.

"My husband is dead." The woman appeared tired and all cried out.

"How did he die?" Cooper asked.

"Shot to death." It was as if she did not want to talk any further; it was all said and done anyway. Cooper had to pump every word out of her by asking questions.

"Who killed him?" Cooper asked.

"It was the hooch runner," said the lady, "he killed him then took the truck. Left me here all alone.

"What happened?"

"When the man brought the jugs, he had a woman with him. A day or two later, he came walking back, saying his truck broke down."

"Was the woman with him when he came back? Cooper asked.

"No, he came walking up to the house all by himself," said the woman.

"Well just what happened, exactly?" pressed Cooper. "And how did you manage to bury your husband yourself?"

"I made the man sandwiches and he was getting ready to leave, when my old man figured the hooch man had money on him, and he wanted it. My old man was shot as he stood in the kitchen and blocked the doorway. Shot my old man dead," explained the woman. "It took me a while to get his body outside where I could bury him. I had to flop him over the wheelbarrow. I'm not a strong woman. It took all day." She moved to sit down on the bench that was on the porch. It seemed just talking about it made her tired all over again."

"My god, you're here all alone now? I can take you into town," offered the sheriff.

"Oh, I'm a tough old bird," breathed the old woman, "although I appreciate your offer, I have hogs, cattle and hens to take care of. My nephews who live across the way have been helping me out with the farm. They come to help me; of course, I already had their uncle buried by then. I'm glad he's gone; I got real tired of him beating me. This here is my farm now to do as I want. Those nephews have their own places and enough work to keep themselves busy, but they help whenever they can. If I ask them to do something for me, it may take them awhile, but they usually get around to doing it."

Cooper was glad to hear that the woman had her nephews to help her if she needed them. The woman also told Cooper that the boys were going to hunt down that hooch man, get the truck back, and get him for killing their uncle.

"Do you have any idea which way the hooch man went, or which way the boys went to look for him?" asked Cooper.

"All I know is they all went down the lane out to the county road. From here I couldn't tell which way they went," said the old woman, drinking water from a tin cup.

The woman insisted on making him a couple of sandwiches and gave him some water out of the well.

Cooper thanked her and said good-bye. He got in his squad car and slowly drove down the lane, which led out to the county road. He had no idea which way to go. He chose to turn left. He just had to guess which direction Jess went. And he had no idea what happened to Mary. He only hoped and prayed that Jess had not killed her, or left her beat up somewhere. He hoped that she was alive and well.

Chapter Twenty-Eight

Back at the Floraville hotel room A1 Joan was all dressed up in her ghostly outfit to scare the heck out of Jess. In the dark she stood at the foot of the bed and gently called out his name.

"Jess," Joan whispered slowly in a singsong way, as she stood at the foot of Jess's hotel bed. "Jess," she repeated again. His breathing changed and he stirred. She saw his legs kick a bit. "Jess, it's Joan." She waited a minute while he stirred in his sleep. "It's Joan, Jess," she sang a little louder, "why did you kill me, Jess?"

All of a sudden, Joan saw Jess's eyes pop open and he stared at the ceiling, then Jess raised his head, and looked directly at her. Joan saw the whites of his eyes; his eyes were large with fright. She wanted to bust out laughing, but she was too angry. The moment perfect! Joan needed to see the fright on his face. He needed to be frightened out of his wits for attempting her murder. Joan knew Jess thought he got away with murder; he strangled her to death and dumped her body into the river.

"Who are you?" Jess's voice sounded shaky and he spoke in a high-pitched tone.

"It's Joan, Jess. Why did you kill me? I loved you so much," Joan said in a slow low mournful way.

"Help!" Jess was squinting now, wiggling, trying to get out of bed, but he was tangled in the sheets and blankets. The more he struggled, the more tangled he got.

"Jess, why did you kill me?" Joan said as she moved closer to the bed.

"Help," Jess tried to scream, but he was choking on his words and made only a whispering sound, "Help."

With lots of thrashing about Jess finally got untangled from the sheet and grabbed his pants on the way out of the door, all the while screaming for help. He ran around the corner into the lobby and passed Mildred staring at him from behind the front desk.

"May I..." She only managed, before he ran out the front door into the street.

"What the hell was that?" Jess was talking to himself, running up and down the street, "just what the hell was that?" he kept repeating, half crying, half laughing. He felt like he was going crazy. And where was his truck? He looked all over. He couldn't find the truck he drove up in. In fact there were no trucks on the street at all. He paced back and forth. Was he going nuts? He knew he left the truck parked out here. And then he heard a voice behind him.

"What's wrong mister. Did you lose something?" Mildred asked she had followed him out the front door of the hotel.

"I can't find my truck." Jess thought he was losing his mind. "I'm going nuts!"

"Oh, come back in and go to bed," Mildred said, playing with him now, "things will look better in the morning, when you sober up." Mildred thought she had him persuaded.

Joan and Mildred about split a gut laughing when Jess ran out the hotel front door, as if the place was on fire. Helen and Ruth had hidden in the hall and were standing with Mildred and Joan now, laughing at poor, pitiful Jess. They didn't want to miss anything and agreed Jess deserved a scary lesson. Mildred wasn't through with him yet, though.

"But lady, I am not drunk," swore Jess, as he followed Mildred back into the hotel front door. Suddenly feeling light headed and tired, he wanted to go back to the room where he had left his stuff. He even began to doubt that he had seen a ghost. He reasoned that it was probably all his imagination or a nightmare. He was too "Yeah, come on back in here," invited Mildred. "It's late, and you can worry about your truck when it gets light. Maybe you parked it in back," said Mildred to an apparently confused Jess.

"You sure ran out of here. Did you hear something outside?" she just had to ask.

"No," said Jess, he felt weird and acted a little ashamed as he stood there scratching his head trying to make sense out of everything. He was a tough guy after all and wasn't going to admit that he had a nightmare or was afraid of ghost.

Mildred offered Jess a cup of hot milk. But he declined and slowly, almost reluctantly, headed toward room A1.

Then as if he suddenly thought of something, he asked Mildred a question. "Say, you wouldn't have another room available would you?" He had suddenly turned around and faced the front desk, and Joan, Ruth, Helen and Mary had to quickly duck down behind the counter again so as not to be seen.

"Oh no, I'm so sorry, A1 is the only room I have available for the next couple of nights. I gave it to you, although another customer wanted to take it. It's everyone's favorite room because the bed is extra nice. I hoped you liked the bed and the room."

"Yeah, ma' am the bed and the room are fine, I guess," Jess told Mildred. He was suddenly feeling faint and knew he had to lie down. So he walked to A1 and laid down after smoothing out the blankets. He was suddenly chilled to the bone and climbed under the covers. He was so exhausted, he fell right to sleep.

Chapter Twenty-Nine

"So, we came to Floraville, and found the truck, so let's go home now," Bart said to Bret."

Bart saw their uncle's truck as soon as they drove onto Main Street. They saw it parked near the hotel.

"Why don't you drive uncle's truck home?" Bart suggested to Bret, "and I'll follow you.

"You mean we're just going to take the truck and leave him be?" Bret hollered at his brother.

"Don't you think we should teach him a lesson," suggested Bret, "for shooting Uncle dead?"

"You know, he probably just abandoned the truck here and got another ride with someone. He has probably hitch-hiked out of here by now," suggested Bart. "Come on, we'll never find him. And you know what?"

"What?" asked Bret.

"We don't know what he looks like, do we now?"

Bart stated as a matter of fact. "We know what our truck looks like, and we got it back. We never saw him, old lady aunt did," Bart reminded Bret. Actually, Bart did remember the bootleggers coming to his uncle's farm, but he was a peaceful man and just wanted the whole ordeal to be over.

"Oh, yeah. Damn," whined Bret, "Damn, we should have brought the old lady with us."

"Come on let's get out of here. Get in Uncle's truck, and head for home and I'll follow you," commanded Bart and Bret did as he was told. Bart wanted to get back home to the old lady; she was out there at the farm all by herself now.

On the way out of town, as he followed Bert, Bart spotted a sheriff's car coming into town, he thought about flagging the sheriff over but then forgot about it because he had the truck and figured the thief was long gone anyway. Besides the man did him a favor killing his ass of an uncle who did nothing but beat his aunt. The man was a jerk and now he was dead. Bart was glad that he was dead.

Chapter Thirty

Mildred, followed by the ladies sneaked around the corner into the hall to room A1. Mildred got down to the key hole and listened. She could hear Jess snoring and it looked like he was sleeping in the dark. They didn't see any light along the bottom of the door or through the key hole.

"Well, ladies, are we all done scaring him for the night?" asked Mildred.

"Oh hell, I want to scare him again," whined Joan. "He deserves it. Remember he tried to kill me; choking me and throwing me in the river like that. And getting away with it, is what boils my blood. The fact that he just got away with it," Joan said sounding very upset. "Why if Helen had not come along when she did, I would be dead." Joan was both angry and sad.

The ladies had agreed, sometimes you just had to carry out justice for yourself. Mary could certainly sympathize; Jess had done her wrong too. She was mad, Jess killed Beau, kidnapped her, and shot at her trying to kill her too.

"Well, what do you want to do next? String him up from a light pole on Main Street?" asked Helen being slightly sarcastic. But she was worried for Joan and Mary's safety and thought Jess was crazy, and crazy people are very unpredictable.

"No, I want to get in there and scare the hell out of him again," said Joan. She just wouldn't let it go. She had to get him back somehow, and she wasn't a violent person so she thought this was her only way.

"Well, what if you did scare him to death this time?" asked Ruth. "Then we would have the body to take of."

"Well, I'll tell you what I would do with the body," declared Joan, "I would take it to the river, wrap fishing line around it and a branch, roll him in and let him float downstream."

Helen, Mary, Mildred and Ruth looked at each other and understood where Joan was coming from. They nodded, and Mildred quietly unlocked the door to A1.

"Get out of my way, I'm going in there," whispered Joan, as she slipped the sheer white material over her head and draped it around until it hung down to the floor. She gently opened the door and could hear Jess snoring loudly. She crept into the room, turned and closed the door behind her, leaving the ladies in the hall to wonder what would happen next. Joan crept down low to the foot of the bed then stood up. Light from the street lamp outside the window cast a glow into the room creating just enough light so he would be able to see "her ghost." *Perfect.* She thought.

"Why did you kill me?" asked Joan in a singsong ghostly voice. "Why did you kill me, Jess?"

When Jess heard his name it was like a light switch came on. Joan could see that his eyes popped open and grew large with fright. The whites of his eyes practically glowed in the dimly lit room. Joan was pleased when she saw them, and almost wanted to burst out laughing.

"Jess, Jess why did you kill me?" Joan said as she began to move closer to the side of the bed.

"Get out of here," Jess screamed. "Get out of here," he repeated and fired off a round from the revolver he held under the blankets.

Cotton fibers floated everywhere in the room. Joan's ears were ringing. She hoped she didn't jump when he shot at her. Ghosts do not jump with fright! Shit! She knew she couldn't run away. Bullets would go right through ghosts. She couldn't show fear, although her insides were shaking as if an earthquake was happening within her. She was visibly shaking and realized that she was lucky he missed her. She knew the ladies hiding outside the door had to worry if she got hit, and she was so glad that they didn't come charging into the room. She had to keep her ghostly appearance up and be brave, so she crept toward him moving closer.

He screamed again which alerted the ladies in the hall that Joan was still okay so they thought they better hide and get away from the door. Jess jumped out of bed, fully clothed, gun in hand, he rushed to the bedroom door, tore it open and ran down the hallway to the lobby. He saw Mildred standing in the lobby. She said she heard a gunshot.

"What's wrong?" Mildred asked and about screamed herself when she saw he had the gun still in his hand. "What is going on?" she demanded.

"I'm leaving this god awful place," hollered Jess as he ran out into the street. He did not looking where he was going, and timing being everything fate could possibly bring him, stepped right in front of Marysville's Sheriff Cooper's car, which was coming fast down the street.

The sheriff didn't see Jess at all. He thought he hit a big rut in the road at first, but somehow it felt different, so he slowed and turned around and looked. The street was dark and it was hard to see, but when he turned around he thought it looked like a body lying in the street. Sheriff Cooper got out and walked a few feet back to where a man lay on his side. He knelt down to take a look, the man looked to be either unconscious or dead. When he turned the man over, he realized that it was Jess from Marysville, the man he had spent days looking for. He was getting down closer to Jess's face to see if he was breathing or not. As he leaned in closer, Jess opened his eyes, saw it was Cooper and shot the sheriff right in the chest. He shot him dead.

The ladies were watching from the shadows of the hotel door. Jess didn't see them, but they saw him leave the sheriff lying there and get up and jump into the sheriff's car and drive off fast, heading out of town.

"Oh, no," they said as they rushed toward the body. "This is not good." He was dead all right.

In a few minutes Floraville's Sheriff Jones ran out to the street to see about the noise. He was at his office where he slept most nights when he wasn't at his cabin at the lake. He had heard the shot and wondered if it was just a car back firing.

Mildred had quickly sent the other ladies inside before Sheriff Jones showed up. She told the Floraville Sheriff that she was behind the hotel desk and thought she heard a shot but she thought at first it was a car backfiring.

"Well how did the Sheriff from Marysville, get here? Where's is his car?" asked Sheriff Jones?

"Well, I don't know," Mildred said looking as confused and strange as the whole night had been so far.

"What was he doing in these parts without a car?" asked the Sheriff. "You heard the shot; did you hear a car pull away?"

"No, I didn't," said Mildred.

The sheriff did not hear a car pull away either. It was a mystery all right, well, to Sheriff Jones anyway. It was a mystery, and Mildred knew the sheriff would probably have to go to his cabin on the lake and do some fishing to think hard about this case before he proceeded with the investigation. She was right. After Sheriff Jones got the undertaker to remove the body, he said he was going to the lake cabin.

***

The ladies sat with Mildred at the hotel until daylight. They felt bad Sheriff Cooper got killed.

"Well, that didn't exactly turn out like we planned," said Mildred. No more creeping around in the dark for them, they had to discuss what their next move was going to be. They realized Mildred could have told the sheriff the man who shot Sheriff Cooper had stayed at the hotel that night. They reasoned Sheriff Jones would have wondered what happened to the man who was run over, if Mildred confessed that she witnessed Sheriff Cooper running over Jess. It was all too complicated. It would have come out somehow that Mary had been with Jess, and Jess had tried to kill Joan, and the ladies did not want to go through all that. They figured Jess was probably long gone by now anyway. They talked it over and decided Jess had probably gotten rid of Sheriff Cooper's car and stolen another car or truck by now and was long gone. They would probably never see him again, but they were wrong.

Chapter Thirty-One

Jess drove out of town and kept driving until he came to another town, called Lensburg. He spotted a nice truck there and decided to drive the sheriff's car into the creek outside of the town. There was a nice steep embankment that made it easy for Jess to push the car over the side and down the embankment. He watched as it tumbled into the creek and sank out of sight. He simply walked back into town and managed to start the motor of the truck he had spotted earlier and drove off with it.

As he drove along the countryside, he got to thinking about that ghost in his hotel room. He didn't think that you could hear ghost breathing, or that the floorboards would make creaking sounds when ghost floated above them. The more Jess thought about it, the more curious he became. He wanted to find out just what was going on. He thought he could disguise himself, after all two can play at this game.

He would grow his hair and beard long. Get a hat and maybe some different clothes. Maybe even dress like a preacher. Yeah, that would be good. He was getting all excited now about the thought of scaring Joan right back. Getting her good. He drove into another town not far off from Lensburg, and bought the hat, shoes and clothes he needed to look like a preacher, one that sold Bibles. Yeah, he liked that idea! So, he bought a couple of Bibles. At night he even read some of the scriptures and passages so he could talk convincingly like a real preacher. Good disguise. Who knows if everything worked out, a preacher would be a great life for him to follow. So yeah, a good plan was put into place. He'd give himself a week to practice selling Bibles around the nearby counties. He would, of course, avoid going to Lensburg for now, because he had stolen the truck from there. No hurry, he would eventually find his way back to Floraville.

Chapter Thirty-Two

The four ladies all went about their jobs. Mary's new beauty parlor was right next door to Helen's dry goods store. And being the only beauty parlor in town, Mary got busy fixing ladies' hair and even cutting men's hair and trimming beards and shaving faces. She liked Ruth's idea with setting up a separate area for a barbershop. The barbershop was in an adjacent room off the beauty parlor with a separate entrance. There were different sounding bells above each door so Mary knew when she was fixing, coloring or permanent waving a woman's hair, when a male customer came in the barbershop for a haircut or shave.

Her plan was to train another beauty operator to help her out, just like she had trained Betty to help her out in her beauty parlor in Marysville, which had worked out so well. She regularly received updates, along with her rent checks. Mary corresponded with Betty by mail, very carefully, just as she always did when she was in

Marysville and she and Ruth sent letters to each other. She knew Jess was out there somewhere and with Sheriff Cooper dead who was to stop Jess from returning to Marysville?

Mary was busy and most of her days were spent working. She lived in the apartment quarters above the beauty parlor and had it fixed up very nicely with the help of Helen's sewing talents. She had new curtains, a lovely bedspread and other accent pieces Helen helped her create. Helen was right next-door as she lived in the tiny apartment above her dry goods store. Joan lived with Ruth and helped Ruth in her pastry shop and adjacent restaurant they ran together. Mildred finally got some dependable help in her hotel who could work the hotel counter at night so she would not have to be there all the time; which freed her up to work in the restaurant she and her son, Jose, added to the hotel. They had hired cooks to help out cooking all day and cleaning the hotel.

Business was good for all the ladies. Floraville was growing and becoming very prosperous and these ladies made a big contribution to its success. There were two banks now, two service stations, new churches, a doctor, and a library. Yes, Floraville was growing, all right.

It was 1925, and prohibition was still the law of the land. The saloon in Floraville was staying open as a restaurant, but people wanted their beers and whiskey, too. People had heard the horrible things about Chicago gangsters and how the Feds came down on them, the newspaper was full of stories of corruption and mob action and the sale of illegal booze. Mary had told the ladies one night at dinner, while they were all together discussing prohibition, she knew how to make hooch first hand because Jess had forced her to help him.

"Oh no, we can't have that!" protested Mildred. "It's too risky; you read the newspapers. If word gets out, if people brag or walk around drunk, they'll suspect us, or the proprietor of the saloon." Mildred protested more, "It would ruin everything." The other three ladies agreed, but they also thought if things began to change, maybe they could do a little business on the side.

"Hey, I just thought of something," Mary added, "only Jess and I know about that mountainside cabin near Marysville with the secret cellar distillery." She smiled, "Just something to keep in mind, ladies."

"Oh no," they all smiled and laughed, "we are busy enough without getting into the hooch business. Besides, it's illegal. Look at the trouble Jess got himself into."

"Speaking of Jess," said Joan "don't you wonder whatever happened to him? He could be right back at that distillery making hooch. And what a great hiding place," smiled Joan "like you said Mary, only you and Jess know about its location now."

"Yeah that's right," said Mary, "Believe it or not. I've been so busy, I actually forgot about Jess these past few months. He is probably back in business selling hooch. Guess we won't have to worry about him anymore."

The four ladies were enjoying themselves having dinner at Mildred's restaurant. After dinner they planned to see a play at the new theatre that had recently opened in town. The ladies all agreed that it was so exciting that Floraville was offering more services and businesses as they looked up and down Main Street on their walk to the theatre.

"Oh, and there is a new church down near the other end of town, I hear. A new preacher is in town, or so says one of my beauty parlor customers," said Mary. Yes, they agreed Floraville was growing, and they were part of its successful growth. It was a peaceful growing town, and the women felt safe living there.

Chapter Thirty-Three

Pastor Josh Roberts was Jess's new religious name, since he had was religiously trained and studied the Bible. He no longer drank the booze he sold, because he realized that being drunk all the time interfered with his business practices. He had turned over a new leaf as he studied under a real pastor and became an apprentice in the pastor's church for six months. Jess alias, Pastor Josh Roberts, was encouraged by his teacher to begin his own church.

Pastor Josh thought it a good idea and decided to add selling booze secretly while beginning a church. He already had the distillery and the distribution route, and now adding his own congregation to the list would bring in so much more money. They would come to him each week at church, rather than having to deliver to them. Pastor Josh was excited about his new plans.

He traded the stolen car in for a new Ford Model T which he playfully called the popular nickname of the day, Tin Lizzie. His hooch sales money came in handy, and he had spent days back at the cabin on the mountainside near Marysville distilling more hooch to sell. What better cover than a church, he thought and it gave him a ready market. Genius! He knew people missed whiskey ever since the Prohibition Law went into effect. Marysville was close enough to Floraville, so it was no problem to go back and forth, especially with a new Model T, traveling was sheer delight.

Yep he thought that he was quite the businessman now, with no time to be in a drunken stupor, he had learned his lesson. He had turned a new leaf. He bought himself a building in Floraville at the corner of Main Street and Ninth. It was easily converted into a church complete with a steeple, a clock and a bell. Rolls of pews were built inside. They were as comfortable as pews were expected to be to keep parishioners from falling asleep as he preached scripture and verse from the pulpit.

It did not take long for the congregation to grow in size. Secrecy was common during prohibition, and Pastor Josh could easily pick out the non-tea tootlers, and in a whisper invited them to come early for a special holy session before services began. He took them down the back steps to the cellar beneath the church, where he kept the special holy water designed to calm your nerves and heal your innards. A few shots before services proved beneficial when the collection plate was passed, and the parishioners felt extra generous. A chosen few were invited with special request to stick around after services, for more of Jess's special holy water, before they enjoyed a fried chicken social lunch held in an adjacent hall. Parishioners were sworn to secrecy. No one wanted to spoil it for everyone else, so they were careful not to say anything or behave totally out of line. This worked out very well because everyone knew the Floraville sheriff was usually out of town at his cabin fishing. Pastor Josh was a business genius, all right. He only had one down fall, and that was when it came to women and one in particular, who haunted him.

***

Pastor Josh was confident that he had it all figured out and no woman was going to get under his skin ever again, like Mary or Joan had. Now that Jess was sober, he pretty much stuck to the business of religion and hooch. He was even somewhat sincere about turning his own life around. And when parishioners had no cash for hooch, he traded hooch for merchandise, if it was something he was interested in. He had sold the deputy's revolver in Lensburg and liked a couple of forty-five caliber revolvers a parishioner offered in trade for booze. He believed in the powers of the Lord, but he was no fool. He thought he would be silly not to have his own power of protection. His motto was, "God helps those who help themselves." He kept one revolver under his pastor's coat most of the time, and one behind the seat in the Model T.

Pastor Josh's long hair and beard suited him. He felt like a new man. Whenever he passed a storefront window he looked at his reflection. He was actually quite proud of himself and the way he dressed in white shirt, bow tie and nice coat, pants and a hat. He was a tall handsome man, and the mirror reflected it to his liking. He actually looked the part of a pastor he thought, and felt at ease as he presented himself as a servant of the Lord.

He was very convincing and when men and women greeted him on the street, he would say hello and tip his hat in return. He bought space in the weekly paper for an announcement and invitation to his church. Soon the members of his Floraville Methodist Church grew and they came every week, especially when word got around in his congregation about the secret cellar in the church. Jess was doing all right for himself between selling hooch from the church cellar, his biweekly hooch delivery route up north, and the generous offerings he received each Sunday morning when the collection basket was passed throughout the congregation. Everything was going smoothly and according to his plans.

Chapter Thirty-Four

The ladies were so busy they had to make it a point to get together to socialize. They took turns going to each other's homes and having pot luck dinner, then playing card games such as pinochle, euchre or canasta. Ruth and Joan's pastry shop and restaurant was doing very well. As was Helen's dry goods store and Mary's beauty parlor and barbershop. Betty continued to successfully run Mary's beauty parlor in Marysville. Mary did not wish Sheriff Cooper to be dead but she hoped that with his death, the search for her was over. She had no idea how many of those wanted posters with her face on it were still out there. And then one day Ruth told her she had received a letter from Betty and wanted to talk to her about it.

"What's in the letter?" Mary asked getting a worried feeling in the pit of her stomach.

"Well, she says don't come to Marysville. There is a new sheriff in town, his name is John Henson, and he is taking over Sheriff Cooper's duties. He's looking for Jess and you, too, Mary."

"What can I do?" Mary asked Ruth, sounding stressed.

"Well disguising yourself is a good idea. You already made your hair darker and you lost weight. Maybe you should go by Marilyn instead of Mary, and don't use your maiden name," suggested Ruth.

"Not Hendricks?" asked Mary, "Jess knows my maiden name, doesn't he? Then how about Hanley?" Mary smiled; she liked the sound of it.

"Yeah, Marilyn Hanley, I like that. Yeah, it is as if I was never married to Beau Jones and sister-in-law to Jess Jones, nor was ever Mary Hendricks. Kind of sad in a way! But Marilyn Hanley is so much safer," agreed Mary, she didn't want the new Sheriff John Henson of Marysville to know where she was.

"There you go," said Ruth, "glad I could help."

Chapter Thirty-Five

Jess Jones took on a new name and profession: Pastor Josh Roberts, he liked that title and it was great cover for his other profession, bootlegging. Everything was going fine; profits were high in both areas. He was happy. Since he became a pastor and returned to Floraville, the ghost of Joan never returned to haunt him. It had been the one thing he was afraid of happening. But it seemed that since he got religion the ghost stayed away.

But still Joan haunted him in a way, because he looked for her in the faces of the women of the congregation. Every Sunday as he stood his church pulpit and preached scripture, he gazed out over the congregation looking for anyone who resembled her. When he walked about town, tipping his hat to the ladies he passed on the street, he looked into their eyes, searching for familiarity. In a mysterious way, it was as if the haunting of Joan drew him to settle his ministry in Floraville. That, and the fact that his hidden cabin with the distillery was close enough to travel back and forth easily enough. He could not go back to Marysville; he knew that there were probably wanted posters hanging everywhere. He thought that wearing preacher clothing and having longer hair and a full beard was disguise enough to fool average folks.

Pastor Josh Roberts decided to spend more time in local businesses, to get to know the town's people better in order to invite them to his church. One day as he was walking down Main Street, the delectable good smells of meat cooking from the restaurant adjacent to the pastry shop, drew him in. An attractive young woman greeted him at the door. She seated him near the window. As he sat alone at the table, he proceeded to write the sermon for the forth-coming Sunday. As he paged through his Bible, thinking of what to write, he saw two women briefly work at the cash register as if training the young lady. When the young lady came back with his bill, he complimented her on the place and the food, and ordered a cheesecake pastry from the pastry shop. As she turned to leave his table to get the pastry, he asked her who ran the restaurant.

"Oh, the two ladies at the register, Ruth and Joan," the young waitress said, turning and looking towards the entrance where the paying station was located.

Josh almost choked on the coffee he was sipping. Well, it could have been another woman named Joan, but he knew it was she. It had to be Joan! Joan was alive? That's impossible! He knew she was dead before he tied her with fishing line to the tree branch and rolled her down the embankment into the river. Jess felt a huge lump in his gut. It was not what he ate but the fact that Joan could possibly identify him although he changed his name and appearance. But even if she did recognize him, what could she do? He could just act like he didn't know her. He couldn't let it go. Was it his imagination? He was being punished; he knew it for killing her and for masquerading as a pastor.

She haunted him ever since she sneaked into his hotel room pretending to be a ghost. How lame was that? He had to get her back. It was the principle of the thing. Joan got on his nerves as a wife and still got on his nerves, just because she was alive. She was still his wife. He decided he had to take care of her for good this time. The thought of her being alive infuriated him. He did not like to fail, and he failed at his attempt to murder her. And he did not like loose ends, and she was a loose end. He had to think of an idea.

The two women were no longer at the register. He was glad to see they were gone. He wanted to make sure he did not run into them, and then he saw them pass by the window where he sat. They were busy talking and did not look inside. He pretended to be writing a sermon as he tried to eat a bit of the cheese pastry, but even though it was delicious, it just wouldn't go down. He had to leave part of it on his plate. He finished his coffee as the young waitress came with the bill and he handed her the money. He got up from the table feeling sick; he would just have to deal with Joan later, he had a church to run.

Jess took a good look at himself in a mirror in the foyer when leaving the restaurant, and he did not like what he saw. Time had gotten away from him, and it had been a while since he had a haircut and his beard trimmed. His hair was all tangled under his hat. He wanted to look good for Sunday's church service. He remembered passing a barbershop that was on the other side of the street, near a dry goods store. So he decided to walk over there to see if the barber could trim his beard and hair.

He looked in the window; the barbershop did not look busy. A man walked out and passed him on the street. Jess thought the man's hair looked rather well trimmed, so the barber must be okay. He gently pulled the door open and heard of the bell tingle on top of the doorframe. He stepped inside, stood and looked around, and then a thin woman with dark hair came around the corner.

"Can I help you?" asked the woman, looking at the man standing in the barbershop wearing a preacher's collar.

"I was wondering if I could have my hair and beard trimmed some, not a whole lot, just a little bit off all around." Jess greeted her with a smile.

"Of course, have a seat right here," she said as she pointed to the hydraulic chair that faced a mirrored table.

"Thank you, ma'am," he was surprised, but pleased to see a woman barber, as he removed his hat and laid it down on the counter.

"My name is Pastor Josh Roberts. I am the new pastor in town," he said as he sat down.

"I see, well welcome to Floraville," Mary replied as she went on to introduce herself. "My name is Marilyn Hanley." She spoke to his reflection in the mirror. The new minister reminded Mary of someone, but she couldn't put her finger on it. She had not met many preachers in her life, being raised without religion as she was. The more she looked at him, the more she thought there was something about his eyes that were half hidden beneath his long hair.

She put the thought aside and went to work putting a cape around him and with her scissors and comb in hand began to trim his hair. She thought she would trim a little off all over and then just ask him if he thought that she had taken enough off. She made small talk about the weather. He tried to make small talk too and said that he had just eaten at the pastry shop restaurant. They talked a bit about the food there and how good it was. He was intrigued; this was his first experience with a woman barber.

"I must admit I was a little surprised to see a woman barber," said Pastor Josh, "and you run the beauty parlor too?"

"Yes, I do," Mary said.

"Nice." He smiled. "I bet that keeps you busy."

Mary thought he looked at her with inquiring eyes

as she responded to his reflection in the mirror. "Is this enough off or should I trim off a little more?" she asked. She could see his eyes better now, and something puzzled her about them, so much that it was becoming hard to concentrate on what she was doing.

"Oh that's fine," Jess answered. He was watching her in the mirror—it seemed as if he knew her from somewhere, but he had never gone to a woman barber before.

"Did you say you run the beauty parlor next door too?" he repeated. For some reason he felt as if he knew her from some time ago, not sure where or when though. He drank so much booze back then, and it had affected his memory. Yeah, wasted days and wasted nights of drunken stupors, and as a result, he couldn't remember half of what he said or did.

"Yes, I do, doing both keeps me busy," said Mary, alias Marilyn, and then they shared small talk about the town growing and getting busier and her plans to get extra help soon. She was concentrating on what she was doing, but she couldn't help but think that his voice seemed awfully familiar. She didn't ask him where he was from, nor did she mention Marysville. It did not take long to trim his beard since he just wanted it evened out.

When she was finished, he said he was pleased. She unhooked and slid the cape off from around his shoulders, then the paper strip careful not to flip the hair trimmings that collected there. She then brushed his neck and turned the hydraulic chair slightly to the left so that he could get up and out of it easily. He already had the two bits and a tip for her in his hand, laying it on the counter. He thanked her as he got up out of the chair and headed toward the door.

"Nice job, Mary," he said as he opened the door and walked out on to the sidewalk.

It took all of five seconds after he left, as she had reached for the broom and began to sweep up hair, for her to realize that he had called her, Mary and not Marilyn, which she told him her name was. She clearly remembered telling him her name was Marilyn. She felt eyes on her. She looked up from sweeping and saw him peering in the window through the big red letters that read "Barber Shop." He stood there looking at her. They stared at each other for what seemed an eternity, but was actually only a few seconds. Tension hung in the air, like a heavy fog making it difficult for her to breath.

He thought the woman looked familiar and that was why he called her "Mary." She stood there wondering if he called her Mary, to see her reaction. Was it Jess? Did he recognize her or was it an honest mistake by this preacher man? And why was this man staring at her? Feeling uncomfortable, she looked down and continued to sweep up the floor. She couldn't look at him anymore, it felt too weird. He wasn't finished with her; she could feel it in her bones. She heard the bell at the top of the door as it swung open. She turned on her heel. She must have had a strange surprised look on her face. Then he spoke.

"I forgot my hat," smiled Preacher Josh.

"Oh." She caught her breath in her throat almost choking, then turned slightly and saw his hat on the counter where he had put it when he came in.

"Thanks ma'am," he said as she handed it to him. The moment felt awkward, as he turned to leave. He put his hand on the doorknob and pulled the door open. "Good day then," he said as he walked out shutting the door behind him.

Mary had to sit down in the chair for a second because she suddenly felt weak and out of breath. She sat for only a second until she heard the beauty parlor bell tinkle above that door. She got up and walked through the short hallway to the adjacent room where her beauty parlor customer stood. She was shaking slightly as the woman sat down and Mary wrapped a cape around her. The woman began explaining how she wanted her hair done and soon all thoughts of the preacher man were put on hold as she concentrated on listening to what style the woman wanted.

It was only later in the evening after her work was finished and she ate a little supper sitting alone in her kitchen, that she realized who the preacher man really was. She immediately gathered the ladies for a meeting at her apartment.

***

"Ladies, I called this meeting because it's been some time since we all had a chance to get together, and I think there is a situation we need to address," said Mary. "And while

I am thinking of it, please remember to call me Marilyn, not Mary, in public." She reminded them.

"Oh, of course," said Ruth. Joan and Helen chimed in, smiling at each other ready to oblige Mary in any way they could.

"It's about Jess," frowned Mary, "I believe that I saw Jess."

"Where?" asked Joan suddenly appearing shaken. "Well, I won't play ghost again. He barely missed me last time. I won't have him shooting at me again."

"I believe the new preacher in town, is Jess Jones, disguised as Preacher Josh Roberts," stated Mary, "seems he and I are both playing a game of charades."

"Oh, no!" exclaimed Helen, and Ruth echoed her response.

"Oh, yes," declared Mary, "he is back. I am almost sure of it. He was cleaned up and sober as a judge, a condition in which I'd never seen Jess—well, not for years anyway. But, I do believe the new pastor in town, at the new church, Pastor Josh Roberts, is Jess. He came into my barbershop for a haircut and beard trim," Mary reported with a shaky voice. "There was something about him, but it didn't sink in until I was finished with his haircut."

"What did he say?" asked Joan. "Did he recognize you?"

"I introduced myself as Marilyn, and he seemed to accept that. So I don't think he realized it was me."

"When I was near finished, he laid his money on the counter with a tip," said Mary.

"Then what?" They all said holding their breath in anticipation and worry.

"Well, he merely got up then and headed for the door."

The ladies sat at the kitchen table looking at each other, thinking the situation with Jess wasn't so bad then. But then Mary added something to stir their very souls.

"He said, 'thanks Mary' as he walked out the door," Mary said with a worried look.

The ladies looked worried now, too.

"You know, I am so used to being called by my name, Mary, that it didn't even dawn on me that he did not call me Marilyn, as I had introduced myself." Mary's voice was quivering now with nervousness.

"I only realized that he called me Mary when I was sweeping the floor and happened to look up to see him standing outside looking at me through the window. You can imagine the fear I felt. I thought he recognized me and was coming back in to physically or verbally attack me," Mary said with a frown.

"Then what happened?" asked Helen, as she and the other ladies sat still, not making a move until they heard the rest of the story.

"Then he came back in," Mary sighed, "and you can only imagine how my heart sank in my chest."

"What happened then?" asked Ruth.

"Nothing, he merely said he forgot his hat. I saw it lying on the counter so I picked it up and handed it to him," said Mary. She took a deep breath before she could go on. The ladies hung on her every word and felt nervous for her.

"He looked at me strangely, I thought. He hesitated a moment," said Mary, feeling weak, "then he turned to leave and walked out the door."

"On, no!" said Helen, Ruth and Joan in unison.

"Maybe it was an innocent mistake," said Ruth, "you know mistaking the name Mary for Marilyn." She added, "You must admit, he is more familiar with the name Mary, since he had known you for a long time and you were with him those days when he was delivery hooch."

"Well, that's true," admitted Mary, "but it also raises the argument that could have made it easier for him to recognize me."

"The question now is what do we do about it?" Ruth looked at Joan, Helen and then Mary. "You two are victims of this evil man. What do you both want to do about it?" asked Ruth looking at Joan then at Mary.

"Well, I have no faith in the sheriff in this town," confessed Joan. "Guess we could hog tie him up and take him back to Marysville."

"Oh yeah, let's tie-up a preacher that everyone is beginning to like and haul him off," said Mary.

Finally, they all agreed they could not do that. If they feared for their lives, and they did, they were going to have to come up with something else. They could hold the hooch business and killings over his head. Blackmail him, as Ruth had suggested, but it was their word against his. Sheriff Cooper was dead and the new sheriff of Marysville, John Henson, would probably arrest both of them.

"What if Jess, I mean Preacher Josh, got religion and decided let bygones be bygones?" suggested Helen.

"You mean maybe he changed his ways after he got religion?" asked Mary looking doubtful.

"Well you never know," Ruth sounded hopeful for their safety's sake.

Can we really count on that?" asked Mary. "I believe he has an attempted murder on his hands—which would be Joan. He killed my husband, his own brother. He killed the sheriff deputy, and the sheriff, and apparently nothing will be done about it. Personally, I can't believe he got religion and changed." Mary was adamant about her conviction.

"I've got an idea." suggested Joan. "Why don't we follow Jess Jones, alias Preacher Josh Roberts, and just see what mischief he gets into?"

They all agreed that was a good idea even though they were all very busy running businesses. They decided they could take turns. Mary and Helen would take first watch and then Ruth and Joan the second. They all agreed following him and finding out what he was up to was a good plan, even if it meant hiring more help temporary in their businesses so they could get time to be away.

***

Mary and Helen had the first watch. They noticed

Josh ate at the usual places two meals a day, but most of the time he hung around his church. He had special meetings with the congregation on Wednesday and then had services Sunday morning.

But there was something odd about his weekends. It seemed he drove out of town on Friday afternoons came back for Sunday morning service, then left town again Sunday afternoon and came back Tuesday evening. They ask people if they had seen the preacher and many reported he did a lot of house calls that took him out of town and into other counties. The ladies believed he was up to something, so they held a meeting to discuss who would follow Jess out of town. Mary and Helen decided they could go. Mary had been instructing an apprentice in her beauty parlor and barbershop so she could take over while she was gone. Helen had hired extra help so she was free to be away, too. Helen and Mary told clients and patrons they would be out of town visiting relatives.

They sat outside of Jess's living quarters behind the church on Friday afternoon when they thought he would be leaving town. They had tied their hair back in buns and wore men's bib overalls and long-sleeve shirts and hats. When they saw Josh get into his Model T and pull out onto Main Street, they waited a few seconds then pulled out after him. The streets were busy with many Model T's and they all looked pretty much alike, so they had to be careful not to lose him by inadvertently following the wrong car.

"There he goes! Go that way Helen," ordered Mary

pointing to the left, her arm extended in front of Helen's face and almost blocked her view.

Jess turned on the road leading to Marysville. But they weren't sure because someone had knocked down the wooden arrow sign at the crossroads. So they just followed him. They tried to pick out something different about his car to distinguish it from all the others Model T's on the road. Finally, the car they were following turned onto a farm lane. They were not sure if it was Jess's car or not by this time.

In any case, Helen pulled over and parked their car behind a grove of trees near a pasture where cows grazed. Helen and Mary got out and crept along the barbed wired fence, stomping through high grass, bushes and trees back to the farm lane, which led a short distance to the farmhouse. There they saw a short fat, gray haired man get out of his Model T and walk to the porch.

"Well, that sure as hell isn't him," complained Mary in disappointment.

"Dang, we lost him," admitted Helen. They headed back to town to sadly report to Ruth and Joan that they had lost him. They said they would really have to pay attention to keep an eye on the driver and not follow another wrong car down the road next time. They had wasted time and gasoline. They hoped Joan and Ruth would have better luck.

***

"So, now it's our turn to try to follow Jess, alias Josh, the preacher man," Joan said, "I hope we have better luck."

Joan and Ruth used Ruth's car and sat in the shade on a Friday afternoon near Jess's home behind the church. They sat there for a few minutes and finally he came out of the door and got into his Tin Lizzie and drove off. Ruth waited a second then followed him. The two women were disguised with their hair tied up in a bun under caps, long-sleeve shirts and overalls like Helen and Mary did. It was their best attempt to not arouse suspicion if Jess saw them. Besides, dressing up in a disguise gave the ladies a sense of intrigue and suspense.

Ruth and Joan both had their eyes stuck on the car about a half-mile up the road. As they drove out of town and other cars and trucks would pull onto the road and turn off. It was busy and they were afraid they would lose track of him. A couple of times when Joan thought that Ruth was driving too closely behind Josh, she would have Ruth make a turn off the road into a farm lane. When he was out of sight they pulled out again, hoping Jess didn't suspect he was being followed. They just hoped it was Jess they were following.

They were at least seven or eight miles from Floraville and getting closer to another town when they saw the Model T turn right into a grassy field between two cornfields. They wondered where in the heck that car was going. They pulled over and waited several minutes before they got out and walked through the corn rows to the grassy field and came upon a flowing brook.

"The tracks stop here, near the field." stated Joan. "Where in the heck did he go?" They walked around a bit, all the while in fear that the car with Jess in it, would return from wherever it went and see them. So they did not stay long before they back-tracked to Floraville. They met up with the Mary and Helen for dinner at Ruth and Joan's pastry shop and restaurant.

"It was the strangest thing," Joan said. "The car just seemed to have disappeared. We followed it all right, and saw it turn off the main road, so we pulled over. It disappeared after it turned off the road onto a grassy field that ran between two cornfields. It went back there and never came out again. The road just stopped."

"Was this in the valley before a mountainside and next to a creek?" Mary asked.

"Yes, it was" said Ruth. "One minute Jess and his car was there, the next minute it disappeared."

"I know where that grassy lane is located," confessed Mary, "When Jess kidnapped me, that is where he took me."

"In the woods? He took you to the woods?" asked Ruth.

"Well, all you have to do is drive to the end of the grassy lane to the creek, then drive through the creek at an angle to the left. Only then you will see beyond the trees and brush, a rutted winding road through the woods that leads up the mountainside. I'd say for about two to three miles, and then almost at the top of the mountain, there is a clearing and in the clearing sits a cabin. That is the cabin where Jess took me and showed me the secret cellar. And the secret cellar is where he had me help him make hooch before we made the run near Springfield on deliveries," explained Mary.

"So Mary, you know how to make hooch?" Joan asked with a smile as she looked around at the other ladies. They smiled too. Yeah, the wheels were turning and the ladies were getting ideas about starting up another business – the hooch business.

"I don't think that new sheriff in Marysville is all that eager to find me, do you?" asked Mary.

"Well if he is into finding you, we'll just pay him off, like the bootleggers pay off the sheriffs in every other county where folks are distilling and selling. It's the Feds who are the ones who are really pushed to uphold Prohibition. And I think they are in Chicago after the big mobs. I heard lots of them were bringing in hooch from Canada by boat and hiding bottles filled with booze in their boots. The law called them bootleggers. I read in the Springfield newspaper that since they built the bridge between Canada and the United States, they'll be sneaking it in secret compartments in cars and trucks, and not only in their boots," reported Helen.

"We don't want to miss out on the action, do we?" questioned Ruth as she looked at the other ladies.

"I can't tell you how many people come into the restaurant and say they wish we had an alcoholic beverage to serve them. Many said they are willing to pay more for the risk involved," shared Joan.

"But what about Jess?" asked Ruth, sounding rather sarcastic. "He'll be cutting into our profits?"

"I bet he's selling it to his parishioners already," suggested Mary. "No wonder I see so many people at his church on Sunday morning."

"You have to admit, he's pretty clever," offered Ruth.

"And a killer," Joan reminded her.

"May I remind you, that he thought he murdered me?" Joan said with a certain look in her eye that told everyone she could easily return the deed. I think I just had an idea. I think I'm going to find a preacher in one of the next towns who is willing to have me under-his-wing so to speak, as an apprentice. I'll learn to take over after Preacher Josh's position, when he isn't around anymore." Joan smiled with an evil grin.

"Why, what's going to happen to him? Where is he going?" asked Helen. They all three looked at her and laughed, and then hugged her. A plan was in place.

So the plan was for Joan to become a preacher and a Bible saleswoman, besides working in the pastry shop and restaurant with Ruth. Mary and Helen were going to keep an eye on Jess as he paraded around as Preacher Josh, but not follow him. There was no need to follow him now, because they knew he was going to the cabin near Marysville every week. They would just learn his schedule. And part of his schedule was stopping at the pastry shop in the morning for cheese Danish and then mid-afternoon for an early dinner at the restaurant.

Joan had Mary restyle her hair—cut short waved into the latest style bob all the ladies were wearing. The latest rage in the roaring 20's, was straight lined dresses, long pearl necklaces, cute little hats with feathers and dancing the flapper and the Charleston. Joan loved her new look. Her hair was darker, and she was thinner than she was before her husband thought he killed her.

Apparently Jess, alias Preacher Josh, did not recognize her when he came into the diner. He didn't act like he knew her—probably out of sight, out of mind. Or maybe he got all holy, reading the Bible he carried with him all the time, and writing those sermons as he sat at his table near the window every day. Maybe, he got religion and turned over a new leaf. But Joan was not convinced of that, because he was still breaking the law distilling and selling hooch. Joan made it a point not to be in the restaurant at his usual eating times, and that worked well for a while.

Chapter Thirty-Six

"Hello Pastor Josh, you are early today," the young hostess said as she looked around to see if Preacher Josh's usual table was available. She smiled because she saw that it was, and then motioned for him to follow her. He smiled and followed her to his usual spot near the window where he could look out at the street and watch the passersby. He smiled and removed his hat as he sat down. He liked to look out the window as he thought of his choice of holy words for Sunday sermons.

The town was growing. There were many more Ford Model T's on the street. The Tin Lizzie was the popular nickname for them. Ford had made the Model T so affordable that nearly everyone bough one or talked about buying one as soon as they got enough money together. The Model T was designed very well with high narrow wheels that went through mud and over ruts quite well. They just needed to pave the street a bit better and the town's street department was working on that. The street was wide and cars parked at an angle and so there was pretty of parking. Preacher Josh was glad the town was growing, that was more business for his church and his secret hooch selling business.

After he ordered his usual meatloaf plate, Pastor Josh looked on as the waitress walked away toward the counter to turn in his order. There were two women working there, they took the order from the waitress and went about preparing it. As Josh watched, he sensed a familiarity about the woman working behind the counter, where the pies and cakes were kept. For a moment he thought he was going crazy with déjà vu.

That woman sure reminded him of Joan. Her hair was different though, darker, stuck to the side of her cheeks, short with deep waves. There was something about her eyes, but more than that, there was something about her mannerisms, the certain way she cocked her head ever so slightly to read an order. The way she nodded and tilted her chin when she listened to a customer ask her a question. He was staring and he knew it, but there was just something about her. Oh, no couldn't be! He brought his attention back to his meatloaf dinner and finished it before it got cold. She walked around the counter to talk to a customer. He watched her; there was something about her walk.

Then he thought about the night he spent in the hotel and the ghost. He admitted he was nearly scared to death. It seemed to him since he had learned the ways of the Bible and was a changed man, Pastor Josh Roberts, he looked at the world a little differently, or did he? Jess Jones was gone, or was he? He tried to push down the angry feelings that Joan brought out in him. How dare she still be alive? Walking back around behind the counter, she glanced over her shoulder in his direction as if she felt his eyes on her. She walked to the kitchen, and he didn't see her again the rest of the time he was there.

After seeing Joan, suddenly in his mind Pastor Josh Roberts was gone and sinister Jess Jones resurfaced. Loose ends and unfinished business haunted Jess. How in the world did Joan survive? He could have sworn she was dead when he rolled her in the river, if not, then she surely would have drowned in the swift current. Of course he realized that he was drunk at the time, when was he ever sober back then? He was well aware Joan could blow his cover, and he was going to have to take care of Joan once and for all. He would make sure that the evil deed was done for sure this time. He just had to figure out where and when.

He almost felt sick to his stomach, when he looked out the window and saw Joan speaking to the woman who worked in the barbershop and had trimmed his beard and cut his hair. *The audacity*, he thought! *She knows I can see her! She just saw me staring at her when she was at the counter.* There was something about the other woman, too.

Pastor Josh was feeling more like the former angry drunken confused Jess. In fact he had never felt more confused; his past was rising up and haunting him, just when he had gotten religion and started a new beginning. He wondered now, was he being punished for his former evil ways or was he just going insane? Had all the booze affected his brain?

The woman standing outside speaking to Joan was Marilyn, the beauty operator and woman barber. *Or was her name Mary?* He wondered if the woman standing out on the sidewalk was not Mary—then, whatever happened to Mary, was she dead? He tried to shoot her when she ran away from the truck. He thought he had shot her, but he never stopped to check for sure. He fired shots in her direction as she ran away from him. There were tall weeds, prairie grass and it was wooded, so maybe his bullet hit a tree? Maybe she did get away?

Jess knew that he was paranoid and never trusted anyone. He was always jealous of his brother, Beau, and that was why he went to get Mary after he killed his brother. It wasn't really that he loved Mary, it was because she had belonged to Beau. But Beau is dead now, by his hand. He felt no remorse! He saw Beau lying dead in the cell next to the dead deputy. He had shot them both. What kind of a man was he?

It all started in an angry drunken rage, when he beat up and choked Joan to death, then threw her body in the river. He felt good seeing her body float away, tied to that big limb, he knew would carry her off and out of the miserable life he had with her. The river swallowed her up and in minutes would dispose of all the evidence. He could still see the image of her body in his head. He wanted to jump up and down with joy at the time.

As Jess watched the two women on the street speak to each other. He thought he saw the woman he thought was Joan motion toward the restaurant window before they stepped out of sight. He just knew they were plotting against him. So what was he going to do about that? They could try to blackmail him, tell him that they would expose his true identity and the fact that he was a lawbreaking drunken murderer. Of course, most of the congregation knew he was a distiller and sold hooch; they were some of his best customers. So how else could these two women ruin him? These women could expose him to his congregation but it was his word against theirs. Besides, they were both alive and well. People would think they were crazy if they came up with a story about him. None-the-less, he knew they were up to something. Jess was so self-centered it never occurred to him that maybe the two women just wanted revenge. Somehow he never associated women with revenge. He thought pretending to be ghost was as far-fetched, as any woman would go. And little did his ego allow him to think otherwise.

Chapter Thirty-Seven

"Jess is inside eating," warned Joan, "I've been coming in to work at odd times to avoid him, but today he came in at a different time than he normally does."

"Do you think he recognized you?" asked Mary looking worried.

"Oh, I think he did," frowned Joan. "Oh, I think he did, all right," Joan sounded concerned.

"I think it's time to engage in a little revenge, don't you, Mary?" asked Joan. "After all he tried to kill both of us."

"So what's the plan?" asked Mary. "We have to do something that will benefit us."

"If we could get our hands on that distillery, we could open a speakeasy," suggested Mary. "We could have lots of business." Mary smiled at the thought and Joan had to smile in agreement.

"Plus it would be lots of fun," agreed Joan. "We could hire some jazz bands. But where do we build it?"

"I think I know a great secret place right next to a hooch source," said Mary.

"And where is that?" asked Joan.

"Up on the mountainside right next to the distillery cabin," Mary said. "We have everything we need there. There are actually three wells for plenty of water, Jess, showed me when he held me captive up there. Actually, only two work and one is abandoned. I wonder if he ever fixed those rotten boards over that abandoned well? He scared me half to death when he pushed me towards it, and I stepped on the rotten boards. The boards shifted and cracked under my weight. I thought I was going in. Then the bastard stood there and laughed at me," said Mary angrily. "I owe him for that one."

"Is there is a fuel generator up there?" asked Joan smiling now. She was getting ideas.

"Yes, a big one. He said he only used half the power of it, and bragged that it could light up a small town if he powered up full blast."

"Better cover up that abandoned well. Sounds like that plywood on it now, is not enough. We don't want people getting drunk and falling in it," suggested Joan.

"Good idea," Mary agreed.

"How do we make sure people who come to the speakeasy, won't be the law or the Feds?" asked Joan.

"They will be selected by special invitation only," suggested Mary smiling at what she thought was a brilliant idea. "In fact maybe we could get people to ride together, and they could meet and park in the back lot at Betty's beauty parlor."

"You know, I like that idea," said Joan. "To make it fun, we could blindfold people and drive them out to the field road, across the creek and up the mountainside to the speakeasy. "

"I like the idea of a mystery trip up the mountainside. It sounds fun. We only have one stumbling block, and that is Jess," said Mary, looking at Joan intently. "Do we cut him in or bump him off?" Mary remembered Jess fired his gun at her which not only frightened her, but made her angry.

"An accident would be great," said Joan, "and I'm just about finished with my preacher apprenticeship with Pastor Hodges, so if something should happen to Pastor Josh, I could easily take over his church and congregation. I think we have a plan, Mary," smiled Joan, "let's see what Helen and Ruth think of it.

***

Mary called a meeting for the next evening. Joan, Mary, Helen and Ruth got together at Helen's living quarters above the dry goods store. When Joan and Mary shared their ideas with them, they were most excited. They talked over how they could include or dispose of Jess, and how they would do it. Mary and Joan had the pleasure to present a not-so-accident accident. They shared their plans and ideas but decided to give it a few days before actually putting a plan into place. Some time to see if the most popular plan still felt right.

Little did they know that Jess had a plan of his own, and was about to strike first.

Chapter Thirty-Eight

When Jess got crazy with a plan, there was no changing his mind. He did not falter with his distillery and hooch delivery plans. And when he got caught, he did not back down or waver but shot his way out of jail killing anyone who tried to stop him. It was how he handled Joan— she got on his nerves so he beat her to death, or so he thought he did. So he would have to be extra careful this time.

He had a plan to sneak into Joan's bedroom where she and Ruth lived behind the pastry shop. Joan was careless about closing her curtains in the evening. So he could easily watch her routine and movements from right outside her window. He would merely cut the screen, crawl in her bedroom and be a ghost to her. He had to laugh. He would get her right back for scaring him like she did, and making a fool out of him. No woman was going to make a fool out of Jess Jones, alias Preacher Josh Roberts. He was going to suffocate her with her own pillow. He had his gun with him; he never went anywhere without it since he saw Joan and Mary talking outside of the restaurant. Oh, he just knew they were talking about him that day, so his plan was to strike first. No one would be the wiser; it would look like Joan died in her sleep.

He had been sneaking around the outside of the house and watching her movements all week, so he knew her routine. He waited until it was late at night. He couldn't believe that he had to kill Joan all over again. This time he would make sure. It was late in the middle of the night, when he crept up to the house and peeked in the windows and found one unlocked.

Jess crawled through the window slowly, careful not to make any noise. The room was dimly lit by the street lamp and full moon. He saw her lying in bed. He crept up and yanked out her pillow from underneath her head then pressed it onto her face and pressed down hard. He pushed harder and harder against her struggles. He pushed so hard he was getting dizzy and heard bells ringing in his head.

It wasn't bells in his head, Joan had bells on her bed and in her struggle managed to grab them and shook them hard, very hard, as hard as she could after she managed to get her hand out from under the covers. Mary, Helen and Ruth, were in the next room like they had been each night for the past week, because they had been watching Jesse follow and watch Joan.

So they were waiting for him to show up one night. In fact they had left the window unlocked to make it easier for him to enter their trap.

The ladies heard Joan ring the bells. She shook them fiercely and frantically, as Jess tried to smother her. Mary, Helen and Ruth rushed to Joan's bedroom door and forced their way in. Mary was the first to get to Jess and she crept behind him and wrapped a drape rope around his neck. She pulled hard; suddenly she became furious and wanted to kill him, so she twisted the rope and pulled it tighter and tighter around his neck. The more she thought of how he killed her husband, kidnapped her, fired shots at her and tried to kill her, the tighter she pulled. Jess was choking and let up on the pillow he held over Joan's face. The harder Mary choked him, the more he eased up on the pillow allowing Joan to wrestle away from him. Quickly she grabbed the gun he carried behind his back in his waistband. Ruth slipped a blindfold over Jess's eyes, as Joan poked him in the ribs with his own gun.

"What's going on?" Jess sounded frightened and angry, as if only he had the right to hurt and torment other people.

"What do you think is going on Jess, or shall I call you Preacher Josh? You think I would just roll over and let you try to kill me again; that I would just let bygones be bygones?" Joan was angry and clinched her fist tight and punched him right in the gut. Jess doubled over in pain. Joan thought it was a good thing Mary had the drape rope around Jess's neck and pulled it tight.

Because if it were her strangling Jess, she would have killed him for sure. This was his second attempt on her life, and she was furious!

"You know I could just shoot you and it would be justified," said Joan, "because this is the second time you have tried to kill me. I'm getting a little tired of it. It's your turn now. What do you say about that?" Joan was sounding very angry, and Jess was actually getting worried.

It seemed for the first time Jess actually realized the seriousness of the situation. Mary wanted to kill him too, and if Ruth hadn't pulled her away and loosened the rope around his neck, Mary might have succeeded. Ruth made sure the blindfold was on good and tight, they stuck a sock in his mouth and gagged him, and tied his hands behind his back, leaving the long rope looped around his neck, as a choker. They had plans for Jess alright.

"Come on Jess," said Ruth, "it's time to go for a ride."

Jess mumbled and squirmed against their tugs.

"For a ride," Joan repeated, "a long ride." And Joan and Helen shoved and pushed him through the house until they got him outside.

They threw him on the back floor of the car and tied him down. Ruth drove, Joan rode shotgun. Mary and Helen sat in the tiny backseat with their feet pressed on Jess, holding him down. The ladies had their plans all mapped out. They were driving to the distillery cabin on the mountainside. It was nearly dawn when they turned off the county road and through the field road, across the shallow creek, and curved their way up the windy mountainside road.

They had a plan. They were building a speakeasy right there next to the cabin and the distilleries so they could make all the hooch they needed for serving folks at their speakeasy.

***

Helen's friend, Joe, was a handyman who did some work in her dry goods store was a trusted friend. He agreed to go to Marysville with her and make plans to build a barn and an addition to the cabin. The barn was to have a nice summer kitchen for cooking when it was hot outside, so as to not heat up the main kitchen in the cabin. The ladies were excited about their plans. It took about three weeks of steady work.

They kept Jess locked up in the cabin distillery cellar that whole time. They fixed him up with all the comforts of home. He had a chamber pot, a pitcher of water, and they passed plates of food under the door once a day. They kept him blindfolded and hands tied when he wasn't eating. They did not trust him; they knew what he was capable of doing. If he got too agitated, they gave him hooch to drink.

Joan took over at his church; the transition went smoothly enough after she finished with ministry learning. She just stepped right in and took over Jess's church, explaining that she was the substitute pastor. Of course, there were no plans for Pastor Josh to return.

The congregation was less concerned about Pastor Josh, and more concerned about getting their hooch, which the new Pastor Joan amply provided. She sold Bibles; she wrote sermons for Sunday morning services. She told the congregation that Jess had to instruct another minister who was starting up a new church over in the next county. The parishioners did not care, they were only too happy to have Pastor Joan. Most of them had come to know Joan at the Pastry Shop where she helped Ruth in the restaurant, and they were happy to have her as their pastor.

The ladies were prosperous and raking in the money. Mary had two new beauty operators in her beauty parlor and barber shop. Helen hired help in her dry goods store to cover for her when she was not there, so she had time to work in the distillery and the new speakeasy. Joan and Ruth's pastry shop and restaurant business was expanding, and they hired more help. All in the all, the ladies provided quite a few jobs for women in Floraville. And now they were going to need help at the speakeasy on the mountaintop.

Times were good and the ladies were ready to have some fun. They had heard talk of speakeasies in Springfield and Chicago with secret doors, secret pass words and secret knocks, and they thought theirs would be fun and mysterious, too. There were no other speakeasies near them in southern Illinois, not within many a mile from Floraville or Marysville.

Ruth met some jazz musicians looking for work in her restaurant. She made room in her restaurant for them to set up and play jazz. They had come from Memphis and were eager to play music for her so she had them play several evenings. She liked their style, a slower blues rich jazzy sound. One evening she engaged them in conversation as they were putting their instruments and equipment away and asked if she could speak to them in confidence about playing music at the speakeasy. They were thrilled at the idea and willing to go along with the secret blindfold trip to the speakeasy. Ruth made a mental note; they were going to need more vehicles waiting for them behind Betty's beauty parlor in Marysville to take all the people to the speakeasy.

***

The time for the grand opening of the speakeasy arrived. They had their private invitations passed out. Joan had selected a few prime parishioners. Mary invited some hair clients with new short bobbed waved styles, who said they wished they had a place to go to show off their new dos and drink and dance, as they did before the crazy prohibition law came about. Ruth got the jazz band together. And Helen notified some of her regular dry goods seamstresses who had sewn women's short slim dresses with fancy fringe trim, bob hats, and made long necklaces to wear with them. The flappers were ready and excited; they looked forward to a fun night,

There were drivers waiting behind Betty's beauty parlor in Marysville. Betty was so excited when she heard the ladies' plans and was more than willing to join in the fun. If the new sheriff in Marysville got too suspicious, Betty knew she could persuade him to back off. He had taken a fancy to her, so he would be no problem. Still the ladies were cautious.

Mary and Joan were already at the cabin and setting things up in the speakeasy.

"Joan did you feed Jess today?" asked Mary. "I forgot, I hope you remembered."

"No, I didn't feed him." Joan was disgusted with Jess and really didn't feel like messing with him. But until they decided what they were going to do with him, they had to keep him in the cellar and feed him. Mary was busy preparing food for the speakeasy grand opening.

"Okay, I'll go down and do it," whined Joan fixing him a plate of ham and eggs. She made sure that she put the revolver in her waistband, and then went down the secret cellar steps to give Jess his plate of food. Joan was only down in the cellar for only a few minutes, when Mary thought she heard Joan scream a gut-wrenching scream.

Then Mary heard a gunshot. Mary dropped what she was doing and ran toward the cellar door. Jess came running up the steps about knocking her down. He looked like an injured wild animal and had blood on his shirt. He squinted his eyes and acted like he couldn't see well; the light in the kitchen blinded him. His face was pale and faded from being indoors so long, his hair was long and straggly, and his beard was tangled and matted which made him look like a wild man. He smelled of sweat and grime as he brushed pass Mary making contact with her arm. He acted like he didn't see her, as if he was blinded by daylight as he charged out of the cabin door.

At that moment Mary was more concerned about Joan. Was the blood on his shirt his or spattered blood from Joan? Where was Joan? Suddenly Joan came running up the steps with the gun in her hand and the look of a murderer on her face. Oh, she was after Jess. This was the third time now that he had tried to kill her.

Jess tore out of the cabin door, with Joan following close behind, and Mary close behind her. Jess stumbled in the yard half blind and bumped into trees. It was as if his legs weren't working after being tied to a chair for weeks. The ladies chased after him and followed him out into the back; he was headed for the woods. He was about twenty feet ahead of them, clearly he was getting away, even though his legs were weak and he stumbled around. Joan and Mary were trying to catch up. Suddenly Jess tripped over something. The ladies heard the crashing of broken boards as Jess fell out of sight. By the time they got up to the well, Jess was long gone. He had tripped over the old wood covering to the abandoned well. The wood had become soft with rot from winter rains and snow and gave way under his weight. Jess was gone.

"Oh crap," said Joan, "let's get the lantern over here." She ran to get a kerosene lamp from the porch; and held it over the opening of the well. It was dark down there and quiet. They fetched a rope, tied it to the lantern and lowered it down into the well as best they could. They could see him. He looked dead, lying down there on his back. The brick well had bricks jagged walls and sharp edges of timber stuck out, too, which he might have hit on the way down.

"What do we do?" Mary asked out of breath from running. She no sooner said it and they were startled by a man's voice behind them. The rope slipped out of Mary's hands and fell with the lantern into the well followed by a distance faint crashing sound.

"Oh, Joe!" said Joan, "You startled us." She gave Mary a sideways glance.

"Hey ladies," smiled Joe, "just came back to get some tools I left here." He looked around wondering what was up.

"We were busting up this wood and going to put new wood over the old dried-up well."

"Well you ladies startled me. I didn't see you over there," said Joe walking towards them.

"Well, we didn't want any animals falling in the well," Mary said getting up off her knees after shuttling some broken boards around over the well hole.

"I got some left-over boards over there by the barn. Let me get a few of those and carry them over there to cover that well."

"You want us to help?" Joan said. She was glad it was getting dark, so Joe wouldn't be able to see down in the well.

"No, ladies, I got it," Joe said as he walked toward

the stack of lumber piled next to the side of the barn. He carried four big pieces and placed them across the opening.

"There, that should do it," said Joe as he smiled and nodded at Mary, but smiled bigger at Joan. He was sweet on Joan and paid more attention to her than what he was doing to cover the well. After he laid down the boards, he turned and walked over to get his tool bag. Then he waved, said good-bye and drove off in his truck. The two ladies stood there watching him and waved back. They looked at each other and smiled.

"Well, that was close," smiled Joan, "and a little creepy."

"Was it? I wonder just how long he was standing over there?" Mary was worried.

"I don't know," Joan was worried, too. "If he saw something, don't you think he would have said something?"

"Well, what about Jess?" Mary asked in a low voice.

"What about him?" Joan had already dismissed him like a dead roach that was bothersome so it got stepped on and disposed of.

"Are we just going to leave him in there?"

"Leave who in where?" Joan asked with a smile.

"Come on let's get cleaned up. We are going to be mighty busy in the next few hours."

The ladies happily shared the duties of bartending, waiting tables, and cooking. Someone shook a little cornstarch on the hardwood floor to all the enthusiastic dancers' delight. Carloads of happy people anticipating the time of their lives arrived, blindfolds were removed, and everyone looked around in awe. The band played, the hooch flowed, and everyone was dancing the Charleston.

Joan, Ruth, Mary, and Helen halfway through the evening, got freed up enough to drink a toast.

"Here's to success," they said in unison. They clinked glasses, laughed and hugged each other. They saluted "woman power" and Joan and Mary winks at each other did not go unnoticed by Ruth and Helen.

"What's up girls?" asked Helen and Ruth in unison.

"Well, let's just say Joan's a widow."

"What?" said Ruth and Helen with puzzled looks.

"Jess had an accident. He was running from the cabin in the dark, crashed through the rotten boards and fell into the abandoned well."

"It's all covered up," smiled Joan, "with new strong boards so no one can happen to wander over there and fall in.

"Then that's it," said Helen and Ruth, in unison.

"Yeah, that's it," agree Mary and Joan.

"Hey, you ladies ready to dance?" yelled a customer who was out on the dance floor shaking a leg with all the other dancers. The ladies went over to join them.

"You ladies sure know how to throw a party," someone yelled.

"Yes, we do, yes, we do." Mary smiled looking fondly at Joan, Helen and Ruth as they danced. She had come a long way since that day she sat feeling sad and lonely in the old faded rocker on the back porch thinking her life in Marysville would never change.

About the Author

This is Dianne Zimmerman's third novel. Her other books, "Emma's Run" and "Jane's Aliens" were published by BookCrafters in 2013 and 2016. Dianne lives in St. Louis and enjoys writing, drawing, photography, running, hiking and road trips.

www.ingramcontent.com/pod-product-compliance
Lightning Source LLC
Chambersburg PA
CBHW050517190726

48284CB00003B/839